D. HARLAN

THEY HAD GOAT HEADS

ATLATL
DAYTON, OHIO

They Had Goat Heads
Copyright © 2010 by D. Harlan Wilson
ISBN-10: 0982628129
ISBN-13: 978-0-9826281-2-6

All rights reserved. No part of this book may be reproduced, stored in a retrieval system, or transmitted by any means without the written permission of the author and publisher.

This is a work of fiction.

Acknowledgment is given to the following magazines, journals and anthologies in which some of these stories originally appeared: *The Offbeat, Shroud Magazine, Mad Hatter's Review, SUB-LIT, The Café Irreal, Steel City Review, Beatdom, Zone 3, The Magazine of Bizarro Fiction, Thieves Jargon, Saucytooth's Webthology, Verbicide Magazine, The Ranfurly Review, Theaker's Quarterly, .ISM Quarterly, Bust Down the Door & Eat All the Chickens, Dark Recesses, Vulcan, The Abacot Journal, Alice Blue Review, Dark Sky Magazine,* and *PANK Magazine.*

Published by Atlatl Press
POB 292644
Dayton, OH 45429
atlatlpress@yahoo.com

Cover art copyright © 2010 by Brandon Duncan
www.corporatedemon.com

Illustrated version of "The Sister" copyright © 2005 by Skye Thorstenson
www.lostheadfactory.com

They Had Goat Heads

ALSO BY D. HARLAN WILSON

Novels

Codename Prague
Peckinpah: An Ultraviolent Romance
Blankety Blank: A Memoir of Vulgaria
Dr. Identity, or, Farewell to Plaquedemia

Fiction Collections

Pseudo-City
Stranger on the Loose
The Kafka Effekt

Nonfiction/Criticism

Technologized Desire: Selfhood & the Body in Postcapitalist Science Fiction

CONTENTS

6 Word Scifi • 1
The Movie That Wasn't There • 2
They Had Goat Heads • 4
Beneath a Pink Sun • 8
Monster Truck • 12
Quality of Life • 13
thot experiment wrtn on ifon • 21
The Arrest • 22
Chimpanzee • 26
Victrola • 29
Whale—with a Surprise Alternate (Happy) Ending!!! • 32
Cape Crusade • 37
Turns • 38
The Womb • 39
Hence the Drama • 40
The Storyteller • 46
Fathers & Sons • 50
Funambulism • 56
Balloon • 58

CONTENTS

The Huis Clos Hotel • 59
The Kerosene Lantern Tour • 63
Lord Byron Circus • 67
The Monk Spitter • 71
Infancy • 74
The Lesson • 75
The Sister • 77
Somewhere in Time • 97
The Egg Raid • 100
Strongmen & Motorcycles
(& Monkeys, Too) • 104
P.O. Box 455 • 106
Hovercraft • 112
Giraffe • 114
Houseguest • 118
The Traumatic Event • 121
Gunplay • 124
Hog Ripping • 129
Elbows & Vestibules • 131
The Burn • 132
To Bed, to Bed—Goodnight • 134

"His wife cries from the rubble, father father, what have you done?"

—Russell Edson, *The Tunnel*

For the Unserious Ones. And for the rest, lip-music: brrrrzzzzrrrr.

6 WORD SCIFI

Mechanical flâneurs goosestep across the prairie.

THE MOVIE THAT WASN'T THERE

I go to a movie and notice I'm starring in it. I don't remember shooting the movie, let alone auditioning for the part. I am not an actor.

Dénouement: A harmless kung fu demonstration threads into a hyperkinetic gorefest. I die, uttering tender, hopeful words into the ear of my wife. A touching moment, despite the impossible carnage distinguishing the scene. People cry.

Credits. Lights.

We file out of the theater and proceed to the cemetery in long silver Lincolns and Cadillacs.

A vast crane lowers me into a hole in the ground. Closed casket. Ribbons of film dangle from the lid, encircling the casket in a corona of celluloid.

The actress who plays an *ingénue fatale* in the movie gives the eulogy. "He w-was the only *reel* man I knew," she whimpers, then makes a sex motion with her finger. The audience nods in painful understanding.

It is a long ceremony. And hot out. Sweat dribbles down my back. Countless grievers speak on my behalf, explaining that, aside from egregious shortcomings, I was a good man. One woman doesn't say anything. She stabs herself, repeatedly, at least fifteen times, possibly more, blood spurting from the wounds, although I can tell she makes a calculated effort not to puncture any vital organs.

An ambulance arrives and two paramedics put her on a stretcher and take her away.

"Fuck you!" she shrieks—at me I think, but maybe not—as the doors of the ambulance slam shut.

Nobody leaves until I have been buried. *Ennui.*

The director shows up at the last minute, just in time to stomp the dirt into my grave. My wife accompanies him. She stands there quietly, staring at her toes.

A gravedigger passes out hors d'oeuvres on the silver platter of an overturned spade.

Chirping. Soft breeze. Smell of fresh air and green pastures. Everybody clasps hands. We run through a field of sunflowers, kicking up our knees. If we fall down, we lie there for awhile and observe the blue screen of sky.

[Insert solar eclipse.]

Dénouement: The reel belies the projectionist's good intentions. It comes loose and he doesn't know how to fix it. White screen. They blame me. And yet reviews of my actions are invariably positive. The only significant critique has to do with my physical stature, a body of lies that doesn't adequately reflect the courage of my character.

THEY HAD GOAT HEADS

They had goat heads ...
 I could see down the hallway from the bed. It stretched two miles into the forest. My mother served me a bowl of vegetable soup. The door was open. I wanted to close it.
 The TV turned on. A goat walked back and forth across the screen. A tall, thin man entered the picture and slaughtered the goat with an axe. The camera zoomed into the man's face. He gazed down at the carcass, eyes wide with terror, mouth creaking open into a chemical scream ...
 The TV turned off.
 A brick crashed through the window. There was a note tied to it. I picked it up and read the note.
 "They have goat heads," it read ... I looked out the window. An astronaut in a bubble helmet and orange spacesuit waved at me, then boarded his shuttle. Liftoff. The motel shook. The shuttle rose like a flag, gaining speed and altitude until it disappeared into the clouds.
 Thunder. The clouds flashed, flickered ...
 The shuttle fell out of the sky, smoldering ... It crashed onto its launch pad and burst into flames. The

They Had Goat Heads

motel shook ...

A door creaked open and the astronaut climbed out. He staggered into a tree and bounced backwards. He looked at the wreckage. He looked at me and took off his bubble helmet. He had a goat head.

I drew the curtain.

Somebody in the ceiling had attached marionette strings to my mother's joints. They had also stapled her lips onto her cheeks. Her teeth were two rows of golf tees. She made desperate sucking noises as the puppeteer compelled her to dust the room and vacuum the carpet.

I heard bleating in the hallway. I told my mother I would be right back.

I shut the door behind me.

For two miles, all of the doors were closed, and I didn't see anyone except a meter maid who tried to take my pulse with a lightning rod. Then I saw an open door. Room 3,401D. I heard cheering inside.

I went inside.

They wanted to play basketball in the boxing ring. Hoops loomed over the ring's turnbuckles. The coaches screamed at each other. The referees ran back and forth and bounced off the ropes, testing their resilience. The players held hands and prayed. They all had goat heads.

I noticed my father in the audience. He pretended not to see me ... I walked up two flights of bleachers and sat by myself.

A referee blew a whistle. Tipoff ...

My mother lumbered into 3,401D. The puppeteer maneuvered her into the boxing ring, scaring away the *dramatis personae*. A microphone descended from the ceiling on a thin length of cord and she gurgled into it.

They played the bagpipes ... I stood and walked downstairs and left 3,401D. The crowd broke into hysterics as I shut the door ... and went back to my room.

I got lost.

I found the lobby. A motel clerk asked to see my room key. I didn't have it. He tried to arrest me. I ran away.

I got lost ...

... timelapse of bellhops and concierges and janitors racing up and down the hallways ... silhouette of the motel set against a blazing horizon ...

I crawled the rest of the way ...

My mother was sleeping in my bed. She looked like a dead seal ... No sign of the puppeteer, and the marionette strings were gone. Open wounds covered her body where the strings had been ripped free. And her lips had been cut off ... I shook her awake and asked her to leave. She made a deflating sound.

Through the window I saw them, thousands of them, tying notes to bricks ...

BENEATH A PINK SUN

Conflict is an illusion without which apes and begonias would shrivel in the wind. The grill, however, is covered with steaks. Tenderloins. They sizzle in the back yard beneath a pink sun. Somebody turns on a bugzapper. Music of tiny deaths. Overweight neighbors in beetle suits scuttle up tree trunks and attack flying squirrels. One should not do battle with arboreal gliders, theoretical or otherwise (ref. Deleuze & Guattari's *Anti-Oedipus*), no matter what they're wearing. Particularly if they lack Just Cause. I can already hear the gavel slamming against the anvil. Blacksmiths line up in the streets and sharpen meat cleavers with power tools. A steel gray Camaro runs them over. Bones crunch. The blacksmiths rise to their knees. An out-of-control stagecoach runs them over. Pastiche of viscera. They stay down for the count as the stagecoach metamorphoses into a giant pumpkin. Remember that old Greco-Egyptian fairy tale of unwarranted oppression and triumphant reward (ref. *Wikipedia*)? Cinderella a.k.a. Rhodopsis was born without a hard palate. She had to install a ribbed prosthesis. She ran her tongue across the prosthesis during moments of ontological skepticism. And yet soldiers rarely strangle each other in the heat of combat. At the same time, keys don't always work. Stick it in a keyhole, turn it ... and it doesn't turn. And you're using the right key. You're sure of it. Inebriation. Hallucination. Micturation. You make a decision to get your back rubbed. Chiropractors invade the Temple of Diegesis and begin cracking the congregation's collective neck. The congregation begs the doctors to stop, but secretly they feel better, fresher. They're thankful for being violated. Near the restrooms, a contortionist juggles minute koalas while dishing out smoked sausages for $3 a pop. Takers are legion, and they're not unhappy with the taste, given the proper medley of condiments. Dip a French fry in ketchup and pretend it's a flaming match. Eat the fire. Ceiling fans have the capacity to burn down the house if you install a flamethrower in the rafters. Acme is the best brand. "I'm extremely happy with this fine product," says a craggy Vietnam veteran and disappears into the jungle depths. Suh-suh-Saigon. Fishermen infiltrate the motels and scale perch in the shower stalls. The manager tells them not to do it, but they do it anyway. Pack of solipsists. They light candles in the hallways, apply blindfolds, strip naked and do fifty yard dashes, trampling old folks who wander into the hallways to get buckets of ice. A blacklight implodes. The baby can't be soothed. It cries and cries and dares somebody to console it. A passenger plane crashes into the apartment complex down the block. Impossible cinematic explosions and carnage. Top notch special effekts. A *daikaiju* (trans. giant monster, e.g., Godzilla) emerges from the electrically charged wreckage and storms up and down the streets of Winesburg. Policemen attack it with harpoons. Ahab impersonators seek pan-seared vengeance. They man the decks of vintage zeppelins. Surprise gust of wind. Queequeg slips and topples over the edge at an altitude of 500 feet. Thud. A bright yellow daisy crawls out of the dirt like an undead corpse (ref. *White Zombie*). A fasttime weed overtakes the daisy like a boa on a flagpole (ref. *Anaconda*, particularly when the great snake vomits a partially digested Paraguayan Jon Voight and Voight winks at Jennifer Lopez and Ice-Cube before dying). The flag comes loose and sails to the horizon like a magic carpet (ref. ول يلة ل يلة ألف ك تاب). Intellect of human viscera. Animé nights and scikungfi battle royals. People paint themselves purple and pretend they're cats. They meow. They drink milk from bowls. They imagine the sensation of possessing an elongated coccyx. Meanwhile the pod door opens and accommodates a heart, pulsing, spitting blood as it floats across the cockpit. "Is it a coincidence?" says Captain Klondike to an off duty space cadet. "Who tears out somebody's heart and throws it into the cosmos?" The space cadet shrugs. The captain fingers his chin. Formica is better than carpet tile, he thinks. Especially in kitchens. If you're going to carpet a kitchen floor, you might as well carpet the stove and the refrigerator, too. And the coffee maker. Got it from Sharper Image. Flavia Fusion J10N. Stainless steel with amazing push-button speed. The payroll clerk assured me that I could purchase this at-home brewing system. I do what the payroll clerk assures me to do. The others lack credibility and élan. That includes fontmakers, of course. All day long they loaf and invite their souls, dreaming up new brands of letters, numbers, symbols. That's no way to spend one's time. Time is precious. Time is the splash of a raindrop on a cornflake.

MONSTER TRUCK

A man wanted to be a monster truck. All day and night, he made vrooming noises and hurled himself over long sequences of beat-up smart cars.

One night he welded giant wheels onto his elbows and knees . . .

"Whoever fights monster trucks should see to it that in the process she does not become a monster truck," said his wife when he tried to crawl into bed. She pointed at the door. The man fell forward onto his wheels and puttered down to the living room couch.

He dreamt of mud-stained windshields, Brobdingnagian engines and sperm whale spoilers . . .

The next morning, the man opened his chest and tuned up his arteries with a monkey wrench. He ate breakfast and drove to work. He drove over his secretary and officemates and his boss. He turned in his resignation and departed in an apocalypse of smoke and skid marks.

On his way home, he swerved into a lamppost and totaled himself . . .

QUALITY OF LIFE

"I have to blow my nose."

I left the office and walked down the hallway to the toilet. The towel dispenser was empty. There was no toilet paper.

I leaned over the sink and pressed one of my nostrils closed. I held my breath and blew . . .

The sink basin overflowed. I looked in the mirror. My mouth was a hideous gash.

I went back to the office. "I have to go to the doctor."

I left.

•

The doctor wore a surgical mask. He claimed to be inordinately susceptible to germs.

I said, "Something's wrong with me."

Raising an eyebrow, the doctor replied, "The weatherman forecasted rain today. Can you believe it?"

The mask garbled his voice. I strode across the room and pulled it off.

He dove underneath a table and begged me to go

Quality of Life

away, coughing and wheezing and choking as if in a gas chamber.

I apologized, and excused myself.

•

The next doctor made me take an IQ test. Satisfied with the results, he asked me why I came to see him.

I said, "Something's wrong with me."

His beard twitched, throbbed ... and crawled off his face. With a squirrel's bare-knuckled urgency, the beard situated itself inside the doctor's white coat pocket like a handkerchief. His smooth cheeks glistened with sweat.

"Pardon me," he droned.

"Ok," I replied, and excused myself.

•

The next doctor opened a closet and sicced a bantam weight wrestler on me. It took me fifteen minutes to pin him. The doctor slapped the floor three times and blew a whistle. The wrestler got up, pulled a wedgie out of his asscrack, and returned to the closet.

Clearing my throat, I stood and asked for a towel.

"Get to the point please," said the doctor.

I sighed. I asked for a milkbowl.

"I have a bedpan." He pulled one out of his coat and handed it to me.

I took it and pressed one of my nostrils closed and held my breath and blew ...

The doctor puckered his lips. He inspected the contents of the bedpan, sniffing, touching, taste-testing them ... He took a picture with a disposable Kodak camera. He disposed of the camera, emptied the contents of the bedpan into a large Ziploc bag and sealed it.

"Wait here please," he said. He locked the door behind him.

•

My nose began to leak of its own free will. I got dizzy and passed out.

A nurse woke me up. "I'm here," she whispered. One of her breasts hung out of her uniform. It sagged down to her knees.

"I'm here too," said the doctor. He pushed the nurse aside. She crashed into a table of surgical instruments. Her breast wrapped around her neck like a tetherball and strangled her. The doctor pulled the errant breast loose and told her to go see the anesthesiologist. She staggered away.

The doctor looked at me. He gave me a paper cup. "Don't let your nose fool you. Your memories are leaking out of your head."

"Memories?"

"Yes. Do you know what memories are? Have you already forgotten?"

I put the cup beneath my nose.

"You're not beyond repair. Allow your memories to drain into the cup. Then drink them. Or don't. Do whatever you want. You don't need memories to stay alive. Quality of life is the thing. I'd like to start you on an antidepressant. Excuse me."

The doctor's head and limbs disappeared into his

Quality of Life

coat and the coat fell to the floor in a clump.

•

My nose stopped leaking. The cup had overflowed and my jeans were soaked. I took them off, stuffed them in a garbage can, and put on a pair of surgical pants I found in a cabinet.

I left.

The doctor passed me in the hallway and pretended not to see me. He was wearing a grizzly bear costume with the head tucked underneath an arm.

I returned to the office. "I'm back." A memo lay on my secretary's desk. It read: "Welcome back!"

I sat behind my desk. The phone rang. I picked it up.

"Hello?"

"It's me," the doctor grumbled.

"Oh. Hi!"

"Why did you leave?"

"I'm not sure. It seemed like the right thing to do. I passed you in the hallway. Why didn't you stop me?"

"I can't answer that question."

"Ok."

Sound of an orgasm. "I diagnosed your condition improperly. I want to refer you to another doctor. I'll send you the prescription for the antidepressant by mail."

"Thank you."

"I have to go."

"Ok."

"Goodbye."

I hung up the phone. "I have to go to the doctor."

Nobody was in the room but me.
  I left.

•

I came back. I picked up the phone and dialed the hospital.
  "Hello?"
  "It's me," I said.
  "I know."
  "I don't know where to go."
  "I know. You hung up before I could tell you." The doctor told me where to go.
  "Ok."
  "Goodbye."
  I hung up the phone. "I'll be back soon." Nobody was in the room but me.

•

Somebody tried to mug me in the elevator. I boxed his ears and smashed his face into the control panel. The elevator stopped at every floor on the way down.
  The referral doctor lived in Singapore. I took a plane.

•

He greeted me with a sensual hug, rubbing his genitals against my thigh. He told me my lips were chapped, offered me a balm and said, "I'm sorry to hear about your condition. Please remove your clothes so that I can see what we're dealing with here."

Quality of Life

I removed my clothes. The doctor studied me. He flicked my penis and fingered my nipples until they were hard. He nodded. "Go ahead and get dressed."

I got dressed.

"Is your nose still giving you trouble?"

I stuck my fingers into my nostrils. I took them out. "No. It's empty."

The doctor smiled. "You're suffering from a rare case of memory loss. It's rare because nobody's ever had it like this before. According to my analysis, you possess no memory whatsoever. Your body, for some reason, has rejected it. Take one of these daily." He handed me a bottle.

I took it. "What's in here?" I twisted off the cap. "There's nothing in here."

"There isn't?"

"No."

"That's curious. But I'm afraid our time is up." The doctor removed a large pair of amputation scissors from a cabinet and asked me to bend over and bare my neck. Unresponsive, I waited for him to depart.

•

On the plane ride home I watched a movie and fingered a stewardess in the lavatory. She gave me free wine. I got drunk.

•

I couldn't remember how to get back to the office. I called my secretary. The answering machine picked up. It said: "We're out of toilet paper. We're out of paper towels."

•

It was raining out. I walked to a store and bought an umbrella. I didn't realize it was a squid on a stick until I tried to open it. Its tentacles stiffened as if electrocuted.

I came to a hill. Tired of walking, I turned the squid onto its head, sat on its underbelly, and rode it down the hill like a sled.

We came to a slow halt in a field at the bottom of the hill. Trees rustled in the wind. Clouds passed overhead. Black-eyed Susans stretched across the field as far as I could see.

A rickshaw ran me over.

•

"You look familiar," said the doctor, inspecting my penis with a magnifying glass.

I sat up on the operating table. "Do I know you?"

His nose had been replaced with a papier mâché elephant trunk. "No," he said. "Drink this."

I drank it. "Goodbye," I said.

The doctor trumpeted.

I pulled up my pants and went home.

•

In my mailbox was a prescription. I took it to the pharmacist. He asked for my insurance card. I gave it to him. He asked for my co-payment. I gave it to him.

Quality of Life

He told a technician to get my medicine. She saluted him, ducked into an aisle and returned with a jar of dill pickles. She handed it to me.

"Dills for thrills," the pharmacist droned.

They said goodbye in unison and a chain-link fence slammed onto the counter like a guillotine.

Grimacing, I twisted open the pickle jar and ate one of the baby dills inside. It was sweet.

•

I fell down. My fingers clenched the pavement.

•

Shadows flowed up and down the streets.

•

I went back to the office.

"I'm back."

There was a note on my secretary's desk. It read: "The sink basin overflowed."

I sat down behind my desk.

I blinked.

I opened a drawer and removed a handheld mirror. I looked in it.

My mouth was a hideous gash ...

THOT EXPERIMENT WRTN ON IFON

the thot experiment went terrily wrong. test subjects suffered & died. hot gore. loVed ones prayed & wept. when it was over, dirty realism littered the epoxy flr of the lab..forenzx was late & the traIl went cld. jrnlists didn't nO wat to write. newscasters eluded cameraeyz. it was bad, bad. underlings marked the outrézone w/yellowtape. the army decLaed martial law & persecuted the indigEnt & any1 who wisedoff. zombie apocalypse. alieN attack. avalanChe of serilkillers..............one man left. the last man. he wud find a way. one gud thot is all it wud takE.

THE ARREST

A man said, "You are under arrest."
 Another man said, "No. You are under arrest."
 "No," said the first man. "It's the other way around. You are the one who is under arrest."
 "I'm not under arrest," said the second man. "You are."
 "I'm going to arrest you now," said the first man, taking the second man by the elbow.
 "No. Now I will arrest you," said the second man, taking the first man by the elbow.
 "Let go of my elbow," said the second man. He agreed to let go, but only if the second man let go, too.
 A third man said, "I'm putting the two of you under arrest."
 "No," said the first man.
 "No," said the second man.
 "Yes," said the third man.
 The first man put the third man in a headlock. He jumped up and down and the third man groaned perfunctorily.
 The second man put the first man in a headlock. He jumped up and down so that the third man expe-

rienced the brunt of two men jumping up and down. He groaned louder, with more drama, yet with less resolve.

"That's enough," said a fourth man. "You are all coming with me. You are all under arrest."

The second man tried to put the fourth man in a headlock with his free arm but the fourth man ducked out of the way. A fifth man snuck up behind the fourth man, wrapped his hands around his neck and choked him to death. Eyes wide with surprise, the fourth man slid to the floor like a raw egg.

The second man released the headlock on the third man. The first man released the headlock on the second man. The first, second, and third men faced the fifth man and the third man said, "You killed that man."

"The three of you are under arrest," said the fifth man.

A sixth man punched out the fifth man. "I'm arresting you." He looked askance at the other men. "I'm arresting all of you, too."

The second and third men attacked a seventh man with tomahawks before he could open his mouth and put anybody under arrest. The seventh man shrieked during the murder. Blood exited his wounds in japanimated spurts as he accused the first and sixth men of allowing him to be murdered by the second and third men.

Weird mucous leaked from the fifth man's orifices.

With his last breath, the seventh man whispered, "I should have arrested you all."

Unexpectedly, the first man took off his clothes and began to make love to his wife. She lay on a cot,

The Arrest

on her back, beckoning him with spread legs and locked knees.

"What does he think he's doing?" asked the third man. The fifth man woke up and the sixth man punched him out again, dirtying his fist with slime. The third man said, "Public sex is an offense. I'm putting those sex offenders under arrest."

The first man climbed off his wife and attacked the third man. They wrestled around on the floor. The nakedness of the first man made the third man increasingly uncomfortable, and he tried his utmost to beat and arrest his opponent without touching him, an impossible feat, technically, and yet within moments, he was in fact beating his opponent without touching him, somehow, impressing all of the other men, except for the second man, who turned to the sixth man and told him that he knew how to beat people up without touching them better than the third man did.

Soon the first man rallied. He grabbed the third man by the ears and cranked his head and snapped his neck. The third man slumped over like a wet pancake. The first man immediately arrested him. Then he arrested the fourth man, the fifth man, and the seventh man.

"You can't arrest dead men," said the sixth man.

"You can't arrest an unconscious man," said the second man.

"I can arrest anybody I want," said the first man.

"No. I can arrest anybody I want," said the second man.

"No you can't," said the sixth man. "I can. I can arrest anybody. I can arrest the entire world."

"I'm putting the world under arrest," said the fifth

man, awakening.

"No. I'm putting the world under arrest," said the sixth man. He blew off the second man's head with a shotgun. "I'm going to arrest the galaxy as well." He turned the shotgun on the fifth man and fired. The fifth man's stomach exploded into flaming tendrils of gore. The sixth man said, "Forthwith I will put every last black hole in the universe behind bars. I will teach Eternity the very meaning of deference and respect and authority. But first things first." He emptied the shells from the shotgun, reloaded it, and put the barrel in his mouth . . .

The first man looked at his wife. She was asleep. "Wake up," he whispered helplessly. "You are under arrest."

She opened her eyes. She stretched, sighed.

She rolled off the bed, slipped into the bathroom and turned on the shower, annulling the voice of her husband . . .

CHIMPANZEE

I forgot to lock the door again. Eventually a chimpanzee swaggered into the house. I called the police.

The 911 operator said, "You have to shoot it. Shoot it now." I told the operator I didn't own a gun. She said, "Then improvise. Stab the monkey with a knife. Bludgeon the primate with a frying pan. Lure the simian into the oven and treat it like a casserole. Do what you must. But do it. Otherwise that hairy interloper may commit a crime. Good luck."

"Wait," I said. I remembered I owned a gun after all. I hung up the phone and went and got it. Loaded it.

I found the chimp sitting at the head of the dining table, polishing mustard yellow teeth with a fingertip. It chirped when it saw me.

I aimed the gun, closed my eyes, and fired . . .

I called the police. "I've just killed a hairy interloper," I said. I was hysterical.

"Calm down, sir," said the 911 operator. "Take a deep breath and explain what happened."

I steadied my breathing, focusing on the operator's voice. She sounded attractive. "Ok. I'm all right. This is what happened." I told her.

"I'm coming over right away," said the operator, and hung up.

I cocked my head. Sirens outside. A knock at the door. I still hadn't locked it.

The door opened and a woman entered and she called my name and marched through the house until she found me, bleak, wild, lingering over the gruesome corpse of the chimpanzee.

"Lower your weapon and step away from the unripe mammal," she barked, fingering a baton. I dropped the gun and backed into a china cabinet. She looked good in her uniform. And she was just my type. Skinny. Young. Like everybody's mother used to be. I wanted to impress her.

"I," I said, pausing for a moment, "have certain powers."

She got on her knees and inspected the chimp, feeling its limbs and neck for a pulse, looking behind its ears for abnormal vascularity. "It's only sleeping, it's only sleeping," she whispered, as if trying to convince herself that reality could be defied, defeated, overturned.

"I blew that thing's brains out," I reminded her.

Cradling the chimp in her arms, she picked it up and rocked it back and forth. "Oh no," she cried.

I said, "I don't usually do this. But would you like to have dinner with me? I'll pay for it."

She accidentally dropped the chimp. It hit the hardwood floor of the dining room like a sack of firewood. She screamed for a long time, then picked the chimp up and hurried away.

Shortly thereafter they stormed into the house and

Chimpanzee

arrested me.

They boxed my ears on the way to the police vehicle. "Abuse is the namesake of certainty," I said.

They pistolwhipped me on the way to the penitentiary. "We mustn't take these things too seriously," I said.

They kicked me into a cell and locked the door. My cellmate was a hairy interloper. "You have to shoot it," it said. "Shoot it now."

But I left my gun at home . . .

A prison guard passed by the cell and began to hammer the bars with a wooden broomstick, accusing us of making a commotion. He screamed and cursed and assailed the bars until the broomstick splintered and broke in half. We stared at him absently.

Two hours later, they gave me my phone call. I dialed 911. The operator remembered my voice. I told her I was about to escape. She said, "Exercise caution as you exit the penitentiary. Jail is a treacherous venue. I advise mankind against prison. Penal institutions belie the contours of sanity. The same logic may be applied to incarceration boxes. Whatever you do, do it asap. Good luck."

I heard a gunshot and the line went dead . . .

VICTROLA

I place the Victrola on the kitchen counter and wait for somebody to get a midnight snack. I hear my mother, upstairs, punctuating the flat notes of birdsongs. I hear my father, too. That rankled snore . . .

Lips sealed, my parents walk into the kitchen holding hands. They see me. They poke around the cupboards, looking for instant coffee. "Decaffeinated," says my father sternly.

I say, "Coffee isn't a snack. It's a drink. It's a pastime."

They turn their heads and stare at me. I realize I haven't said anything.

They give up and go back upstairs and the catastrophe of their discord recommences, instantly. Inhuman melodies forced from two strangled radios . . .

I wait, listening . . .

Finally somebody makes an appearance. A stranger. He wears a three-piece suit and a stovepipe hat that scrapes across the ceiling as he strides toward the refrigerator. I engage the Victrola, placing its needle on an old record. The record is warped and produces harsh static before articulating these words: "Welcome to the kitchen. I am your host. I hope you enjoy a snack. You must enjoy things. Eventually you will die." I mouth the words as they yawn out of the machine's *fleur-de-lis*. The stranger stops in his tracks and regards me with wide, unblinking eyes. He sucks in his cheeks. The Victrola says, "You look hungry. You should eat something. If you are not killed in a freak accident, eventually your body will eat you. Cancer, you see. Our bodies always eat us in the end." I continue to mouth the words. The stranger removes his hat and sits on the floor.

My parents return. They dance around the stranger and rifle through the cupboards again. They think that if they look hard enough a jar of decaffeinated coffee crystals will appear, somewhere, behind something, even though I know there is no coffee in the house, and they know it, too.

They give up again. "That's life, son," says my mother, tilting her head. "One failure after another. But one must continue to fail. Otherwise one ceases to be human."

My father grabs her violently and jerks her from side to side. He pushes her over and wrestles with her on the kitchen floor, ripping buttons from her nightgown. The stranger observes the skirmish idly.

Winded, my parents get up. My father takes my mother in his arms and they slip away . . .

Upstairs my mother's tune changes: she shifts from the flat notes of birdsongs to the emotional drones of power ballads. And my father's snore gives birth to hundreds of minor snores.

. . . This is the climax. The stranger knows it. I know it. The Victrola confirms it, saying, "I am very pleased to meet you. You are diseased. Goodnight." I remove the needle from the record as the stranger lies flat and curls into a languid ball. I watch. I listen to my mother and father's muffled voices. They intersect and accomplish a crescendo, then roll out and taper off, fatigued, paling, until the only thing I can hear is the hush of ocean surf, the Victrola's *fleur-de-lis* whispering like a conch.

WHALE—WITH A SURPRISE ALTERNATE (HAPPY) ENDING!!!

My daughter wanted a goldfish. I said, "We can do better than that."

I took her to the pet shop and asked a clerk where the whales were. She escorted us through a maze of aisles into a separate room, pausing to reprimand a stock boy who had stolen a nap. My daughter gazed wide-eyed at the caged lizards, birds, insects, monkeys that we passed *en route* . . .

"This is what we call the Whale Room," said the clerk. She made a sweeping motion with her arm. "We also have an Elephant Room and Brontosaurus Room. The dinosaurs aren't real." She gave us a hand buzzer and told us to press it if we needed anything.

Excusing herself, she closed and locked the door behind her. My daughter and I looked at each other, then at the Whale Room.

It was the size of an airplane hangar and smelled like a bowl of cereal. "Golden Grahams," said my daughter, nodding. I told her cereal didn't smell like anything unless you got really close to it and sniffed very, very deeply. My daughter said, "That's silly, Daddy."

The concrete floor was immaculate and had been cleaned, lacquered, and dusted. An aquarium the size of a two-story house stood at the far corner. There was nothing else.

I put my daughter on my shoulders and we walked to the aquarium.

The bluegreen water glowed with toxicity.

A copious layer of fluorescent cow and pig skulls had been spread across the floor of the aquarium. Aggressive algae-eaters darted in and out of the eye sockets and jaws, unhinged for lack of any food other than their own regurgitated stool.

There was no whale.

My daughter began to cry.

I pressed the hand-buzzer. Nobody came. I pressed it again and again and again. My daughter cried harder and I told her not to worry. "Things always work out, somehow."

Finally the clerk attended to us. I assumed it was the clerk; she was far away and I didn't have my glasses on, and she put on an ornate gas mask as she approached the aquarium. She spoke to me through a contraption resembling a CB radio, holding the microphone to the mouth-chute of the mask. A cord attached the microphone to a long, cumbersome speaker she held at her side like a suitcase.

"Good afternoon," she said when she reached us. The greeting boomed out of the speaker and echoed across the Whale Room. "It is a pleasure to see you again."

I put my daughter down. Sniffling, she cowered

between my knees. I stroked her hair reassuringly and said, "Don't worry, little girl." I looked at the clerk. "You're frightening my daughter. What is this?" I gesticulated at the aquarium.

Harsh sledges of static punctuated the clerk's subsequent monologue: "Ah yes, I forgot. We had to submit the mammal for repair. Too many potential buyers requested to see inside of the mammal. All of the potential buyers said the same thing: 'We won't consider purchasing this unit unless we can see inside of it.' So the owners of the pet shop had a meeting and decided to install a series of zippers onto its vast girth. 'Consumer thirst must be slaked,' they said. That's exactly what they said. This decision was made only recently and we only recently sent it away. You should have seen me duke it out with the mammal; I pushed its head back into the wall with both of my hands while monstrous tidbits fell from its mouth to the floor. For a moment I thought we had become friends. But the whale quickly reminded me that we would always be enemies, biting off my arm." She showed us her arms, one at a time. Neither arm had been bitten off. "Well. I promise the whale will return soon. In fact, we expect to receive two additional units, all of them equipped with zippers that might be opened and closed in a highly user-friendly manner by courageous scuba divers. In their absence, perhaps you could exercise your imagination. Tell yourself the whale is there. The mind cannot deny what you tell it."

The clerk bowed awkwardly and excused herself. We watched her walk away, across the expanse of the Whale Room. She walked slowly. It took over two minutes. She tripped once, dropping the speaker. She got up and tripped again when she tried to pick the speaker back up—I suspected it was much heavier than it looked. Then she disappeared through a thin rectangle of door.

My daughter and I held hands and stared at the aquarium. "Don't believe that horseshit about imagination," I told her. "The real thing is always better. That's why the imagination exists. Mostly, people can't get the real things they want. So they have to pretend."

The algae-eaters threaded through the skulls. They seemed to multiply before our eyes as they devoured crumbs of excrement . . .

It took some convincing. But eventually my daughter talked me into it.

We stripped to our underwear and climbed a ladder that ran up the aquarium's exterior, its rungs cold and sharp on the soles of our feet.

"I wish we had snorkels," my daughter said.

"Lungs are good enough," I replied. "Remember to take a deep breath."

At the top was a small square platform. We situated ourselves on it, pinched our noses, counted to three, and jumped in . . . We sank to the bottom, smiling at each other even though the water stung our eyes. The algae-eaters scattered as we landed on the skulls. They were slick to the touch, like warm balls of oil—we handled them, and we got tangled in them, and we slipped through them . . . There was nothing we could do. We fell deeper and deeper into the colored bone . . .

As we disappeared from sight, my daughter pointed overhead, excitedly, as if to acknowledge the extraordinary passing of a cloud.

Alternate (Happy) Ending

The algae-eaters threaded through the skulls. They seemed to multiply before our eyes as they devoured crumbs of excrement ...

"I'm hungry," said my daughter.

We went home and grilled hamburgers. Big ones. I grilled them and then we sat on a blanket in the back yard and grinned deliriously at one another as we ate.

CAPE CRUSADE

A man wanted to be a caped crusader. He put on a cape, stuck out his chest, and called his alter ego "The Cape." But the cape itched, especially around the collar. He adjusted the collar. He scratched his neck. Nothing worked. And so the cape became his arch nemesis. Like a dog chasing its tail, he pursued the cape, running in circles, trying to grasp its Fabric of Evil ... He grew dizzy. He stumbled onto a bridge and fell over the railing.

"The Cape!" said a man from below, pointing ...

TURNS

They took turns using the scalpel. By dawn, they had successfully severed my feet from my ankles, my hands from my wrists. I stopped screaming. I started screaming again as they began to sew my hands to my ankles, my feet to my wrists with a crewel needle. As always, they took turns. When the operation was over, I cleared my throat, did a handstand, and gestured at the clock with my toes. They frowned at each other, then yawned and turned off the lights.

THE WOMB

A child's mother wouldn't allow him to crawl back into her womb. He cried an ocean of tears.

"The world hurts," the child had said.

"I'm on my period," the mother had replied.

And so he began to cry. He cried for years, bobbing like a cork in the surf of his misery.

Finally the mother rowed out to him in a boat. "My period's over," she explained. "But the answer is still no."

Somewhere a daydream possessed a hummingbird. Flying at top speed, it exploded onto a windowpane . . .

HENCE THE DRAMA

I was shopping for Hawaiian shirts in the clearance section when a clerk appeared with a red phone on a platter. A bird's nest of bobby pins held her hair in place. I looked back and forth between the hair and the phone.

The phone rang.

"It is for you," said the clerk in an eastern European accent.

The ring was loud. Shoppers glanced in our direction. I wasn't entirely sure the clerk was talking to me, even though she had addressed me squarely, even though she was looking right at me, holding the phone out to me, and I was looking at her, and looking at the phone, but still, I couldn't be sure ...

She smiled. Long crow's feet sprung to attention, redefining the arch of her cheeks. "It is for you," she repeated.

There was no cord.

I hung up the shirt I had been inspecting and picked up the phone.

"Hello?" said a voice. "Hello? Is this you?"

"Who is this?" I said.

"There's no time for that," the voice replied. "I'm just glad it's you."

"Who are you?"

"In five seconds you're going to hang up the phone. Then something bad will happen." Five seconds passed. "Ok, hang up the phone now."

I listened . . .

The line went dead. I hung up the phone. The clerk thanked me and walked away, trying too hard to swing her hips.

She came back as I was slipping into a shirt covered with bruised, wilted flowers. This time she wheeled out an old television set on a metal cart. She had let her hair down; it spilled over her shoulders in kinked tendrils. "This will happen now," she said, turning a knob on the TV. I glanced over my shoulders to see if anybody was watching me. They weren't.

Nothing but silent peppersalt on the TV. I buttoned the shirt and waved my arms in circles to test its flexibility. Too tight. I unbuttoned it.

The clerk eyeballed me. She had lost all of her color. I thought she might pass out.

The peppersalt dissolved into a commercial and the sound came on. I couldn't be sure what the commercial was attempting to sell. In it, a thin man in a white hospital uniform demonstrated how to yank a tooth out of a stranger's mouth using household tongs. He spoke gibberish but somehow I knew what he meant. He stood on a busy street corner. Strangers passed by and at calculated intervals he tackled one and put him or her in a sleeper hold. After they passed out, he pried open their mouths and, as promised, yanked out a tooth, usually an incisor, but sometimes the front teeth, and once, amazingly, a molar. Blood surged from the resultant wounds and the strangers woke up screaming and ran away holding their mouths. The man stood, smoked a cigarette, gibbered at the camera. Then it happened all over again.

The clerk turned the TV off after the sixth attack. "Mind you, he is an amateur dentist. But one can't deny the virtue of his product."

I listened . . .

"Violence happens every day," she croaked in a forcibly possessed tone. "Nobody knows why. People live and die and are forgotten. Nobody cares. And yet people want answers. Hence the drama of human existence."

Ignoring her, I said, "Do you have this shirt in a larger size. The shoulders are constricting. The larges in this brand are like mediums, I think. Can you check on that for me?"

"Let me check on that for you," she said. Her tone was normal now. She took the shirt and draped it over the TV and wheeled it into the changing room.

I spent twenty minutes looking at shoes. I needed a new pair of sandals. They had been arranged on a narrow set of shelves that rose to the ceiling of the store. I had to use a ladder to look at them all. Several pairs caught my attention, but whenever I reached for them, someone shook the ladder from below. It was a different person every time. Nobody looked familiar. I climbed down the ladder again and again to confront them, but I was far too slow, and by the time I reached the bottom, they were gone.

I wandered up and down the aisles searching for the clerk. I couldn't find her. I asked another clerk where she was. He asked me to describe her. I said she was a woman and that's all I remembered. The clerk nodded and excused himself.

Tentatively, I crept into the changing room.

It was bright. I had to shield my eyes.

I moved forward, hunched over, squinting, struggling to bring things into focus. I acclimatized slowly. I heard voices. Panicked voices. Breathing. A few cheers.

The lights went out. The changing room fell silent.

I listened . . .

I moved forward . . . down a dark hallway, feeling the walls. They were cold, like ice, but not quite like ice . . .

I passed through a door into a vast amphitheater.

I could see well enough. There were at least 100 people sitting in the audience, including the glitterati in the balconies.

A circle of light fell onto the empty stage.

Nothing happened for awhile. Then an SUV rumbled onto the stage, spun out of control, and crashed into a support column. A man exploded through the windshield and tumbled, with a certain lumbering grace, onto one knee, arms outstretched, blood coursing from his gored forehead. He wore a disheveled brown suit and struck an eerie polyphonous high note. He paused, and struck another note. And another one, and another one. No microphone—his voice was powerful and carried across the amphitheater like rolling thunder. At first I thought the notes were letters, and I thought the letters might be spelling out my surname, but like so many things, I couldn't be sure . . . I concluded that the notes didn't mean or say anything;

Hence the Drama

they merely went up and down and up and down with no apparent purpose or direction or *dénouement* ... In time the man passed out. He fell forward and his chest and face hit the floor of the stage with a crack of bones and wood. Nobody clapped. The circle of light expanded until the entire stage was in view and a movie screen descended from the ceiling, slowly and mechanically.

An old 35 mm projector sputtered to life.

There was an advertisement for coffee.

There was an advertisement for lard.

Then the main attraction: a pornographic film called *Makeshift*.

The clerk stood awkwardly in an empty park, naked except for glossy black boots and gloves. Blonde wig. Her breasts heaved above a stomach of stretch marks. Birds chirped in the treetops. She looked into the camera with glazed eyes and her mouth half open. A man with an erection entered the scene. It was the amateur dentist. The hair on his chest and stomach was long and feathery and looked fake. He carried bloody household tongs. I listened. The clerk turned sideways, placed hands on knees and spread her legs. Concerned whispers from the audience. The amateur dentist positioned himself behind the clerk. He pinched the flesh of her thigh with the tongs. She bit her lip. He spanked her ... and entered her. Clapping. I listened. The actors didn't make any noises. Minimal facial contortions. The amateur dentist repeated the same mantra, sometimes in German, mostly in English, at calculated intervals:

"Hence the drama ... Hence the drama ... *Foglich das Drama* ... Hence the drama ... "

Stiff breeze. The leaves of autumn fell all around them. Beneath the movie screen, the singer bled to death, his rich substance expanding across the stage. I listened, I listened ... Rupture of eardrums. The amateur dentist reached climax. The clerk grinned, thanked him. He pushed her aside. He threw himself on her, forced open her mouth and yanked out her teeth, one at a time. She screamed until her larynx burst. Then died. The amateur dentist stood and stared at the camera and finally walked off screen ... Credits. The lights came on. The audience left the amphitheater. They ambled through the changing room and into the department store, exchanging polite comments and talking about clothes they might buy. Behind them, a teenager in a red striped shirt swept the aisles with a straw broom.

THE STORYTELLER
"Based on a True Story"

When he finished telling the story, he left my office.

He came back, told me the same story, and left again.

He came back again and told the story over, pausing to emphasize the importance of attention-grabbing introductions.

He left.

He came back a fourth time and told the story over, twice, back to back.

He left. He came back.

Halfway through the sixth elocution I said, "I think I've heard this story before." He continued to the end as if there had been no interruption.

He did a clumsy pirouette and reiterated the story.

He left. He didn't come back . . .

I looked at my computer. New email. He had sent me the story as .doc, .rtf, .pdf, and .wpd documents. He had also embedded it in the body of the email. "I hope you enjoy this story," read the subject box. I deleted it. My phone rang. I answered it.

"I just sent you an email," he said. "In case you

didn't receive it, I wanted to tell you something." He told me the story.

He hung up and sprinted to my office . . .

"Hello?" I said into the phone. "Hello? Hello?"

"Hello," he said, standing in my doorway, and told me the story . . .

I nodded.

I made understanding faces.

I smiled.

I made surprised faces.

I pushed out my lips.

I nodded again.

. . . He finished the story, turned to leave, came back and told the story, turned to leave, came back and told the story and told the story and told the story, turned to leave, and left.

I looked at my desk.

A hole formed in my office wall. A drill bit leapt through the hole. "Psst," he said, then told me the story. Afterwards he slipped two small rolls of paper through the hole that, unfolded, revealed the story— one in shorthand, one in Sanskrit.

I put a square of duct tape over the hole. I turned off my computer. I closed and locked my office door.

There was a knock at the door.

I didn't say anything.

There was another knock.

I said, "Nobody's in here."

He said, "But the sound of your voice indicates a source, i.e., voices don't come from nowhere, or, in this case, nobody."

I agreed with him.

"Open up," he reminded me.

The Storyteller

I unlocked and opened the door.

He told me the story. He was about to repeat the story when I said, "Yes, yes. It begins like this, then that happens, then it ends."

Confused, he told me the story. I fell asleep during the climax. He woke me up and asked if I needed him to repeat the climax.

"I can tell you what happens in the climax," I said, prompting him to repeat the climax. Then he backtracked and told the story from beginning to end. He shouted the words of the *dénouement*. I put in a pair of earplugs. He slapped me across the face and the earplugs flew out. I stood defiantly. He implored me to calm down and take a seat. He apologized.

He told me the story.

I told him my wife and daughter were expecting me at home.

He told me the story.

I told him I was hungry and had to go.

He told me the story. He told me the story.

I told him he had told me that very story, like, twenty-one times today, not including written accounts, and not to mention how many times he had told the story to me the day before, and the day before, and the day before …

He replied, "At the end of Time, in the anus of Entropy, when the universe burns out and all the stars turn into black holes, the only thing left will be my story."

I told him I disagreed; other people told stories, too. I also wondered how his story might survive in the wake of human oblivion.

He said it was my right to disagree. He said it was

human nature to wonder about things. Then he said, "Now listen to this." And told the story. And told it again. And again, and again. Over and over. And over again . . .

Eventually he grew tired.

His neck gave and his head tipped to one side, to the other side.

His shoulders slouched.

His voice cracked and got raspy.

He fought the urge to fall to his knees.

On his knees, he fought the urge to fall to his stomach.

On his stomach, he whispered the story, with resolve at first, but his voice gradually petered out as his eyelids weakened, flickered, closed . . . He continued to mouth the story in silence for a few minutes before slipping into a deep, catatonic sleep, at which point the story may or may not have played out in his dreams, rerun after rerun, like a doorbell that goes on forever, like a curtain that perpetually rises and falls, daring the audience to set it on fire . . .

Before leaving, I called my wife and told her about my day. "He kept telling me this story," I said. And in the calmest voice she could muster, she replied, "I know that story, darling. We're waiting for you."

FATHERS & SONS

"Dad's dead," said my father. "I better put him in the freezer."

Grandpa lay on the kitchen floor, tightened into a fetal curl. He looked like a crumpled sheet of sandpaper. Dad picked him up and slung him over his shoulder and went downstairs.

I waited.

He came back later. "Dad's in the freezer. I had to fold him up to get him in there. But he's in there."

I didn't know what to say. "That's good news," I said.

He made himself a ham sandwich with American cheese. No condiments. I asked if he would make me a boloney sandwich. No cheese. He made me a peanut butter and banana sandwich. As he sliced the banana into long, precise rectangles, he explained how fruit had not always been as readily available at the supermarket as it was nowadays.

The sandwich tasted good.

"Oh."

I stopped chewing. "Did you hear that?"

Dad shook his head. "No."

"Somebody said 'Oh'."

"Ohh."

"There it is again."

"There's what again?"

"That 'Oh' sound. It's coming from the basement."

"The basement," Dad echoed, and clucked his tongue.

I put my sandwich down. My father finished his sandwich and poured a tall glass of milk. He drank it and wiped the milk mustache from his overlip with a shirtsleeve. He licked his overlip and wiped it again. Licked it again. He scrubbed it with a dishtowel. "It won't come off!"

I squinted at him. "I don't see anything."

"Ohhh."

"I better go check on that." He put the towel down and put some Chap-Stick on and took a bite of my sandwich and said "Mmm" and went downstairs.

I waited. Much longer than last time. I looked at the clock and tried to figure out how long my father was gone. The hands of the clock taunted me, dared me. But no matter how hard I tried, I couldn't figure out what they meant.

He came back later, covered in dirt and sweat. His T-shirt was ripped in places. He hurried over to me and finished my sandwich in two great bites. "That tasted so nice," he said.

"I'm glad you enjoyed it."

"I'll make you another one. I promise."

"I believe you."

"I've just been thinking about that peanut butter and banana sandwich for awhile, is all. Since I made it for you."

"It's not a problem."

"I know." He smiled for a long time. His neck looked stiff. I felt awkward. Then his head sort of slumped off-kilter and the smile became a slot.

"Your grandpa's dead," said the slot.

"What happened?"

"He's dead. People die. It just takes time, sometimes."

"Ok."

He looked at the clock, then at me. "You need to learn to tell time."

"I can tell time."

"What time is it?"

I studied the clock. "3 a.m.," I said in a casual, uncaring voice.

"Not quite," said Dad. "It's 12:30. In the p.m."

"Hm."

"It's light out, for Chrissakes." He pointed at the window.

I looked out the window. "I know."

"You're a big boy, goddamn it. Learn to tell the damn time."

"Ok."

"How old are you? You're pretty old to not know how to tell time. You're like in your thirties or something."

"I'm not that old."

"You're old enough."

"Ok."

"Ok, ok. It's settled." He shrugged. He shrugged again, holding the shrug at its summit. He let his shoulders fall and shrugged once more. "By the way," he said, "Dad got out of the freezer. He looked hurt. We wrestled around on the dirt floor. He told me I was a bad son. 'Don't ever tell your son he's bad,' I told him. He apologized and said he didn't mean it. I said not to worry about it and we wrestled some more. Then I bashed his head in for awhile with a two-by-four until he stopped moving and squirming around. He lay there like the empty husk of a goddamned Junebug. I dug a hole with a garden hoe and nudged Dad into the hole with my foot and then I filled the hole back in. We need to get a gravestone. Write that down. They sell them at Wal-Mart for, like, really cheap. We also need to get the basement carpeted. Dirt floors are bullshit."

I stared at the crumbs on my plate.

"Don't be sore," said my father. "He would've died eventually. I think he was dead. I think it was just a reflex or something."

"Ohhhhhhhhhhhhhhh."

"Jesus Christ! What the fuck is this? A fuckin' fairy tale?" Dad looked at me expectantly.

"What's a fairy tale?" I said.

"Jesus." He took off his T-shirt, looked down at his belly and studied it. Grey, bristled patches of hair marked the flabby mass. "Jesus I'm getting fat. Jesus H Christ."

"Ohhh."

I said, "I think Grandpa's alive again."

"I'll be right back." He poured two shots of tequila and we toasted to Good Times and slammed them. Then he went downstairs ...

Five days might have passed. Maybe five hours. Or five minutes.

At some point I noticed Dad skulking through the kitchen. He had retrieved Grandpa and was carrying him in a Baby Björn. Grandpa's thin, pale, liver-spotted limbs dangled lifelessly from the apparatus. He looked very clean, though: Dad must have washed him in the basement sink.

They went to the back yard. I went to the window and cranked it open. The fresh, summer air smelled good.

Dad took Grandpa out of the Björn and told him to go play. Grandpa didn't respond; he lay on the grass as if poured there, eyes half open, ribcage slowly rising and falling. One moment Dad scolded him; the next he encouraged him. Then he put a leash on Grandpa and started dragging him around the yard. Now and then Grandpa tried to keep up, but he was too weak, and for the most part he could only let himself be dragged. His face and scalp turned purple.

One of the neighbors came over. I didn't know his name. He wore red longjohns and construction boots. He had just killed a deer and wanted to show my father. He brought the carcass over in a wheelbarrow. He explained how he had "destroyed" the deer with his bare hands. He kept repeating the word "destroyed." At first he and the deer merely wrestled in a playful manner, but things got dirty. The deer tried to run away but tripped over a fallen pine tree. The neighbor jumped on it and punched it in the head until it died. "Luckily it was a doe and there weren't no antlers on it," he said. "Otherwise I mighta cut my fists when I destroyed that crazy fucker."

Dad said it was a nice-looking deer, despite its mauled, almost unrecognizable head. The neighbor thanked him.

Grandpa gasped for air. He convulsed for lack of oxygen.

The neighbor wheeled the carcass back into his yard and began to skin it with a hunting knife. One strip of deerhide after another he tossed over his shoulders. The musculature of the deer was bright red. Fluorescent. It looked fake.

Dad pulled Grandpa around the yard a few more times, falling into a soft trot. Then he came back inside and lay Grandpa on the kitchen counter. His neck was inflamed, bruised and bleeding. I checked his pulse. He was alive. We stared down at him.

"I'm thirsty," said Grandpa.

Dad made a frog face. "Thirst is part of life. People get thirsty. That's life."

"Respect your elders," said Grandpa.

"Fear your offspring," said my father, eyeballing me.

I offered Grandpa a shot of Tequila. He wanted water. I got him a glass of soda and carefully poured it into the gash of his mouth as if filling up a lawn mower with gasoline. He choked on the soda but managed to get some of it down. "That wasn't water," he remarked, then rolled onto his side and tightened into a fetal curl.

FUNAMBULISM

I insisted they replace the tightrope with a two-foot wide plank before walking across it. I also wanted the plank bolstered from the underside by a series of pillars and support beams. In addition, I wanted three nets set up—one near the ground, one halfway between the ground and me, one just a few feet beneath me, all made of spidersteel and reinforced with a Tungsten nanocomposite—and a strongman waiting to catch me beneath the third and lowest net in case I fell through them all. "Secure my path with handrailings, too," I added, and then I realized there was no reason to walk across the plank when I could glide across it. I ordered them to construct an airport walkalator instead of a plank. "Make it four—no, five feet wide," I said, putting on a sumo suit in case I fell down. I put on another sumo suit for good measure. And I decided that, instead of pillars and support beams, they should fill the circus tent with sand, fill it all the way up here to the tightrope platform, and then we can simply lay the walkalator on top, but since we're on the subject, why use sand when we can use concrete? I barked, "Fill the tent with concrete!" and began to gesticulate as if my hair had caught fire. I quickly checked myself, however, and demanded that they not only fill the tent with concrete, but the whole city. Frenzied, they assembled a mountain of gravel bags and water barrels and loaded up a battalion of cement trucks. As they leapt into the trucks and revved the engines, I reneged. "Forget about the concrete. Forget about the sand. Just make sure that walkalator is stabilized. Please wrap it in cellophane as well. I don't want to get any germs on my feet." I took off the second sumo suit. I took off the first one. I thought twice and put them both back on. I added a third. I took all three suits off and put all three back on again as they erected pillars and set up nets and hired a strongman and designed and assembled a walkalator, which they summarily laid atop the pillars from one platform to the other, sealing it in place with miniature blowtorches, and they even ran a series of copper wires from the walkalator's handrailings to the ceiling, ensuring that it wouldn't budge. "A brontosaurus could fall on this walkalator from the roof of a tall building," the foreman said, "and it still wouldn't budge." I thanked him. He climbed down the ladder and left me alone. The spotlights came on. The crowd grew quiet and stared up at me. Beneath the nets, the strongman flexed his pectoral muscles and exclaimed, "Don't worry! I'll catch you if you fall!" I waved at him. I waved at the crowd. I took a series of deep breaths, waved at the crowd again, smoothed out my eyebrows, cleared my throat, scratched one of my earlobes ... Finally I stepped onto the walkalator. It ushered me from one platform to the other without incident. Halfway across I did a masterful cartwheel. The crowd cheered.

BALLOON

It wouldn't deflate. In fact, it had grown larger and more buoyant. I purchased it over three months ago and it continued to float there, adamant, proud, its string tied to an armrest and taut as a guitar's. The balloon was daring me. I decided to stick it with a knife. It absorbed the blow, as if expecting it, and the balloon dimpled and wrinkled as it sunk to the floor. My daughter thought it was dead. She insisted that we bury the carcass in the back yard, near the garden. We invited guests, my daughter and I. There was a long ceremony followed by a catered lunch. Everybody talked about the balloon, remembering the good times. Nobody talked about how I had gotten away with murder.

THE HUIS CLOS HOTEL

Marionette puppet in the corner. Long strings rose into an obscure grill in the ceiling and I couldn't see who was manipulating them. I heard heavy breathing up there. Sometimes sharp curses.

The puppet stood eight feet tall with long shoulders and piercing features. It wore a gray suit and held a paperthin paddle in a wooden hand. Imprinted on the paddle was a photographic headshot of itself, or rather the man who had served as a blueprint for the puppet. At random intervals, the puppet raised the paddle to its face and repeated the same mantra in an electric monotone: "No strings attached."

I opened an umbrella as more and more guests strode through the lobby. A bellhop sneered at me. He conferred with another bellhop who conferred with a doorman. The doorman pointed at a check-in clerk and gestured at me. The check-in clerk blew a whistle and a concierge appeared at my side, chin upturned.

"Today I met the man who will take out my gall bladder," I said, tilting the umbrella to one side. "He seems like a good man."

The Huis Clos Hotel

The concierge didn't say anything. I noticed a small, inconspicuous fishhook protruding from the close-shaven flesh of his chin. Its line rose into an obscure grill in the ceiling.

"They say that the Huis Clos Hotel is where everything happens," uttered the concierge through tight lips. "I regret to inform you that an important part of everything is death."

I closed the umbrella and eyeballed the puppet. Its puppeteer yanked on the strings attached to its shoulders, producing a vulgar shrug.

I looked at the concierge. His head jerked up and down and he turned toward an elevator, toes dragging across the carpet.

Reaching for a chandelier and striking an aggrieved pose, I faded out of the narrative like a *nosferatu* at dawn . . .

. . . All of the elevators in the hotel dinged at the same time and the doors slid open and a troop of boy scouts in hunter green knee socks and hunter green shorts and khaki shortsleeve shirts with red neckerchiefs exited and got into formation and marched through the lobby citing their Law in unison: "A scout is trustworthy, loyal, helpful, friendly, courteous, kind, obedient, cheerful, thrifty, brave, clean, and reverent." They repeated the Law until the last scout had exited one of eight revolving doors, the hotel's only entranceways. Staff and guests alike acknowledged the procession with three-fingered salutes.

A woodpecker flew into the lobby through an open skylight. It landed on the puppet's nose and began to jackhammer its forehead. It pecked a quick hole and ruptured a pipeline; glowing antifreeze exploded from the wound. The puppet staggered backwards into the wall, shooing away the bird with pinwheel swats, trying to plug the wound with its fingers, but the antifreeze kept coming, spurting across the lobby. Guests slipped and fell. Staff members tried to help them up and they slipped and fell, too, waving their arms in awkward circles even after they had hit the floor, stranded on the paisley carpet.

Commotion in the ceiling. Like a stampede of tap shoes and cowboy boots moving across an old, rickety stage. It shifted all over the lobby, erratically, with no apparent direction or purpose. The puppet followed the commotion, wigwagging and hemorrhaging, as if being jabbed with broom handles from multiple angles. He trampled the concierge. He trampled a family of four. Outcries, accusations. Everybody threw up their arms in feigned slow motion. All the while the puppet continued to put the paddle to its face and articulate its mantra ...

The puppet collapsed in a revolving door, jamming all eight of them—the entranceways functioned as a hive mind—and its marionette strings snapped. The puppeteer blew a hole in the ceiling with a shotgun, dropped a thick rope through the hole, and rappelled down it. On his head he wore a small cardboard box with rectangular eye-slits. Seven or eight men wearing the same boxes followed him down the rope. All of them wore gray suits. As more and more people struggled to get inside the hotel, congealing on the sidewalk into an elastic riot, they piled onto the eight-foot obstruction and scrambled to set it free.

A fire started.

Arson. The guilty party slipped onto a fire escape

The Huis Clos Hotel

and bolted the door behind him. Nobody could get out. Everybody caught fire.

Final images: ... The burning face of a man with long shoulders and piercing features turned to ashes. The roof caved in. Suns and moons timelapsed across the sky ... The ashes blew away, revealing a large, herbaceous pinecone with scales that twitched and glistened in the ruins.

THE KEROSENE LANTERN TOUR

The kerosene lantern tour lasted for eighty-six days. They showed us the wick. They discussed the lantern's agricultural application. They compared its candela of light to a firefly's mating call.

When the tour guides ran out of material, they escorted us to a cliff and ordered us to leap off. We used plastic garbage bags for parachutes.

At the bottom of the cliff, a morbidly obese woman contemplated an abortion. She leaned against a rock, folds of bruised fat expanding from her core. "I'm three hundred and one and a half months pregnant," she groused. Her jaw hung open like a laundry chute. "This is a big one. I don't eat much. It's genetic. I will explode with baby flesh if somebody doesn't help me."

Somebody began to beat her with a horsewhip. The woman sighed convulsively with each lash. We watched for awhile, commenting on the whipper's skill, acuity, and experience as a corporeal instrument of torture. Then we jumped on the whipper and wrestled the horsewhip away from him.

We climbed back up the cliff on the rungs of exposed roots and tree branches. By the time we had reached the top, twenty-three days later, the tour

The Kerosene Lantern Tour

guides had thought of something else to tell us about the kerosene lantern. "Observe the curvature of its porcelain trunk." They moved their hands in a synchronized arc. "If you confiscate the glass housing, one might easily mistake the contraption for a vase. One might attempt to arrange flowers in such a contraption."

An ant bit me on the foot. My pupils engulfed my eyeballs. "I am the flesh-bot through which the ant speaks," I said. "I can turn this flesh-bot into a GIANT ME if I like." I fell to the ground and scuttled toward a pile of dirt. They captured me in a burlap sack, hung me on a tree branch, hit me with golf clubs, injected me with something cold, and cut me loose. I felt better.

"And now we shall communicate entirely by way of interesting aphorisms and twice-told tales," said a stranger.

Dazed, I didn't see who had spoken. Everybody looked at me as if I were the culprit.

Then everybody commenced trading aphorisms and twice-told tales . . .

The end of human machinery is the beginning of timeless lint blizzards.

A cautious man always eats the bait before he catches the fishes.

Timeless lint blizzards should be wrangled and punished with the same efficiency and enthusiasm as cautious men. The fact is . . .

. . . Lithuanian tourists cannot be trusted. Nonetheless he survived. His subsequent epiphany produced a fiery mean-on. Figuratively and literally. He buttered up the natives with a few Molotov cocktails, then razed them with a flamethrower. Their ashes floated across the water like decayed barcodes. The end . . . Lithuanian tourists cannot be trusted. Nonetheless he survived. His subsequent epiphany produced a fiery mean-on. Figuratively and literally. Thus he buttered up the natives with a few Molotov cocktails, then razed them with a flamethrower. Their ashes floated across the water like decayed barcodes. The end . . .

They passed around a bowl of string cheese. We were instructed to take no more than two servings apiece under the penalty of excommunication from the kerosene lantern tour.

The gears of the clock tower looming over the reservation slowly rusted and died. Nobody fixed them.

We killed an elk. Nobody ate it.

We wrote a play and tried to perform it. Nobody could remember their lines.

We observed a group member's bald spot with magnifying glasses, speculating about its origin and future. Some of the children began to cry; they had to be timeouted. Music emanated from a broken Victrola. Voices disambiguated. The arrows pointed NNW. The color turquoise went extinct. A man's navel exploded. *Kaiju* emerged from the surf. Gunfire. Extended lectures on pedagogy. Ultraviolent Amerikan Dreams. They wanted to sell the land and build a suburb, but protestors egged the developers and yanked down their trousers. Conversation oscillated between guttural squawks and heated meditations on beef eating. 1001 nights in Bangkok. Antennae. Pulp morality. Darkness.

The whipper cracked his knuckles and said, "It is

The Kerosene Lantern Tour

time for bed. Hence we must lie down. No man owns the right to remain erect and awake when bedtime has come to pass."

... At sunup, we rolled off our cots and shuffled around the kerosene lantern like drowsy penguins. The tour guides didn't get up until noon. They negated their hangovers with makeshift IVs. They smoked cigarettes. They did calisthenics, screaming at each other to go faster.

Pulsing swaths of clouds contaminated the sky ...

They instructed us in the realm of nomenclature. "Some users call it paraffin," said a tour guide, "whereas others simply refer to it as The Wet Substance that Bursts Aflame When One Touches It with Fire ... "

LORD BYRON CIRCUS

Polar bears inundated the Midwest, walking on hind legs and willing to work for below minimum wage ... The penguins shed their tuxedos and picketed until dusk. The migrant workers went home and ate breakfast. The pterodactyl men pulled up their pantaloons and ran to the DMV, shrieking like moths and requesting dire audiences with the Secretary of Hate ... Something happened to the parataxis man. He slipped and fell from a cliff and landed on his head but he was all right and he got up and dusted himself off and looked both ways and a steel-eyed bull nailed him in the tailbone. He flipped end over end back onto the lip of the cliff in a casual standing position. Meanwhile the polar bears were stealing everybody's jobs. They operated at the very pinnacle of efficiency, pausing only to use the Men's Room and devour the odd assistant manager ... "The technology of the mechanized retroflesh," said a backyard fetishist in response to an organ donor who asked him for the time and directions to the cafeteria ... (NOTE: The connections don't work. A work ethic isn't enough to excel in the postcapitalist scheme of intelligent design.) ... Down

Lord Byron Circus

the hallway Judge Schreber slipped out of a straight jacket, snuck up behind a sunflower, and strapped the jacket onto the perennial beast's green limbs. The sunflower resisted, seeds and florets erupting from its oversized head like sparks. Just last night Judge Schreber sentenced a Venus flytrap to two years in Auschwitz for eating more than its lawful share—EIGHT FLIES PER TRAP PER DAY OR ELSE, say the Rules of the Game—and now here he stood oppressing yet another member of the plant family. A wildly anabolic sense of guilt induced an epileptic seizure. He hit the floor and vibrated and clanked like a rusty turbine. Clock springs exploded from his ears and nostrils and then his flesh gave way to the Machine, sharp follicles of metal growing from his pores in fasttime until he became a porcupine of conductivity and industrial panic, a *tetsuo* through and through. "That's unwise," said a hole in the blackface of the sunflower. A polar bear said the same thing when it discovered its boss making love to the candy bar dispenser in the break room. It didn't know what to do. Quit? Or ride this gig to the end? It cleared its mind and searched for an answer ... nothing. Best consult the *I Ching*. The polar bear dumped a bag of yarrow stalks onto the table, carefully arranged them according to the schiz-flows of its psyche, then consulted an out-of-date translation of Lao-tzu's *New York Times* bestseller. This is what the book told the animal:

> *When taxes are too high,*
> *people go hungry.*
> *When the government is too intrusive,*
> *people lose their spirit.*

D. HARLAN WILSON

Act for the people's benefit.
Trust them; leave them alone.

The candy bar dispenser groaned as the polar bear's lips flared with gray blood ... Life as nothing more than the struggle not to shout expletives at Black Tie Luncheons. Life as nothing more than the shouting of expletives at Red Lobster when the food comes out and the depressed-emaciated-browbeaten waitress breaks down and cries mascara-stained tears all over your Seaside Shrimp Trio because her husband's in the clink and her snaggletoothed kids have low self-esteem and too many VDs ... Breakfast at Tiffany Texarkana's. George Peppard is there and so is the rest of the A-Team. After the gangbang a machine-gunfight breaks out. No blood. Nobody gets shot and everybody dies ... "Don't forget to boil that nipple!" exclaimed Mother as she tiptoed across the balance beam. Father saluted and thought: Who serves a perfectly healthy infant a cold nipple? Then the acrobats began to spill out of the ceiling ducts in a somersaulting tsunami of hard-boiled aggression. The gymnasium filled up quickly. Mother and Father escaped through an emergency exit. Infant was left behind and grew up to be a comic book villain ... (NOTE: Don't forget about the polar bears.) ... Neglect is the fundament of psychopathy. Schreber'll tell you. Freud, too ... Consider Freud's analysis of Schreber via his memoirs: "The exciting cause of his illness, then, was an outburst of homosexual libido; the object of this libido was probably from the very first his physician, who enjoyed masquerading around the asylum in various polar bear costumes." ... That's when everybody started goosing and trying to fuck the animals. Bestiality became the apple of the working man's eye, but humanality wasn't the polar bears' bag. They clocked out, collected payment for services rendered, dropped back onto all fours, and returned to the North Pole where the sun raced around the horizon like a tangerine in a blue, blue toilet bowl ... In their wake, the gears and girders of existence fell into an abrupt Romantic stupor. Pistons, cogs, engines sang in the cornfield breeze as the Lord Byron Circus emerged from the dust and tore across the landscape of the Midwest going 120 mph. Celebratory terrazzos of gore hung out the windows of the mechanical centipede that served as the circus's caboose. Taking the lead was a virgin mime who had yet to officially parody the wiles of men in the public sphere. His vast goosesteps progressed forward in a deafening, technologized blur ...

THE MONK SPITTER

There was a machine that spit monks. "Ptk," went the machine. "Ptk. Ptk."

Brown bundles of fabric sailed across the sky . . .

A police force patrolled the field to make sure the monks didn't break anything when they landed. For instance: A monk hit the ground face first and swallowed a mouthful of dirt and a policeman helped him up by the elbow and patted him on the back so he didn't choke on the dirt and the monk dusted himself off and thanked the policeman and the policeman asked the monk if he had broken any bones and the monk felt his body from top to bottom to top and told the policeman he believed his bones were in good shape. Nodding, the policeman folded arms across chest, and the monk said, "If you think about it, all white people look vaguely like Macauley Culkin. The skin. The lips. This is assuming, of course, that all white people have blond hair. Likewise must they possess a certain undernourished quality."

Next: The clouds fell into the horizon, exposing an unforgiving red sun, and all the monks pulled down their hoods, and the policemen pulled down the brims

The Monk Spitter

of their hats.

Next: One of the monks noticed a small tear in his hood. He brandished a needle and thread and sewed up the tear.

Next: ...

Next: An old man took a sip of hot bouillon.

The bouillon tasted sour, and the old man died of malaise, but not before writing a letter to the bouillon factory that produced it. The letter read: "I'm extremely saddened by your bouillon."

Next: ... Dunno. A violent shipwreck?

The *S.S. Buzzardspoon* crashed into a towering island reef at a speed exceeding 80 knots. Bar tenders, lounge singers, captains, navy seals, smokestack sweepers flew off of the deck and were impaled on a vast, otherworldly bed of stalagmites. Death throes. Spurts and rivulets of gore. The native islanders swarmed the carnage like termites. Colonists must be taught a lesson. Frozen screams. Sequence of apocalyptic explosions. A kraken rose out of the surf and devoured the natives by the handful. Sopwith Camel warplanes sputtered overhead and dropped bombs the size of mules. More explosions. One of the planes flew into the kraken's cyclopic eye and the beast toppled over with a resounding grunt. Across the universe a meteor spiraled into a black hole. On the other side of the island a second ship, the *S.S. Yanomamo*, crashed. No stalagmites here. No boulders or rocks. Only a smooth white coastline—and yet the *S.S. Yanomamo* still, somehow, crashed. Every soul on board survived. They dashed to the island's highest peak and erected a church with steeples and bell towers and gargoyles and the pastor slammed his fist into his palm and the congregation took communion and spoke in tongues and put on capes with collars that swallowed their heads. In the vestibule, children poked each other in the ribs. In the belfry, an arthritic hunchback swung on a bell clapper like a monkey. In the basement, a stranger wolfed down his medication and waited, patiently, for the pain to subside.

In the distance: "Ptk" . . .

INFANCY

A man screwed an antenna into the soft spot of an infant's skull and tried to get a signal. No luck.

He called the front desk of the hotel. "The baby doesn't work," he told the concierge. "I'm getting rid of it." He hung up the phone, opened a window, and honored his promise.

The shriek of radio static dopplered down to the street . . .

THE LESSON

The lesson-giver's elbow wasn't working. Whenever he thrust his finger into the air to accentuate a point, the elbow convulsed, swung like a pendulum, and struck him in the cheek. His audience: a morass of taxidermists imitating ornery, cigar-smoking bullfrogs.

Nearby a tree shook its leaves. Everybody pretended the tree wasn't there ...

The lesson-giver grew more careful. He thrust his finger softly, gently, and his elbow began to kiss him on the cheek. A taxidermist acknowledged the feat of acclimatization with a powerful *ribbit!* The tree acknowledged it by shaking its leaves harder.

Overhead the silhouette of a kung-fu fighter sailed across the night sky. His karate chops were as fluid and true as a child's mother-love ...

The finger stopped thrusting, the elbow stopped kissing. The taxidermists swallowed their cigars and stood as the elbow blackened, withered, died. It fell off of his arm and swam to the earth like a leaf.

The lesson-giver pushed out his lips. "Let that be a lesson to you," he croaked ...

THE SISTER

Illustrated by Skye Thorstenson

He used **FLORESCENT YELLOW** yarn to tie her to the grill of a monster truck.

"You be careful", I said to the stranger, grabbing a fistful of air. "I just fixed her, and I don't want to fix her again."

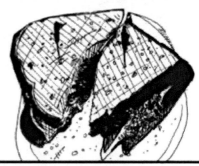

"What I want is to be left alone so I can make a descent sandwich.

Is that too much to ask? I'm sick of this."

Not knowing how to respond, the stranger looked at me and squeaked like a dolphin.

I blinked.

The stranger climbed into the driver's seat of the monster truck.

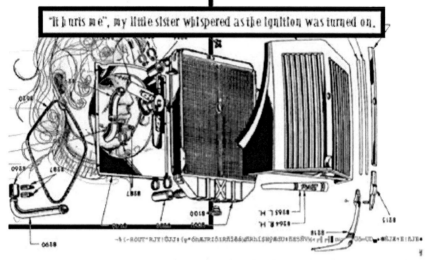

"It hurts me", my little sister whispered as the ignition was turned on.

I wondered what she meant by "it" -- the hot steam that was leaking out of the trucks grill, or the stitches I had used to tie her flesh back together.

fuck my hand HURTS

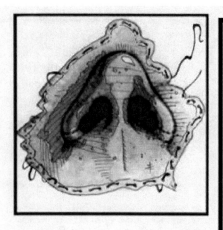

Her nose came loose and fell off.

The stranger rolled his window down and casually waved goodbye to me. I told him to mind his manners.

He told me to mind my own business, and floored the gas. The monster truck was going about 80 mph when it ran head-on into the brick wall.

Not bad for such a big rig.

The wall exploded when the truck hit it. So did my sister. Bricks and body parts erupted into the emerald sky in slow   m   o   t   l   o   n...

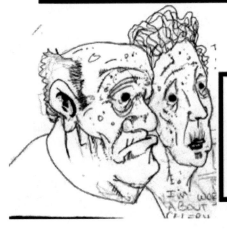

The stranger slammed on his brakes. He turned off the ignition, hopped out of the truck. Admired his dirty work.

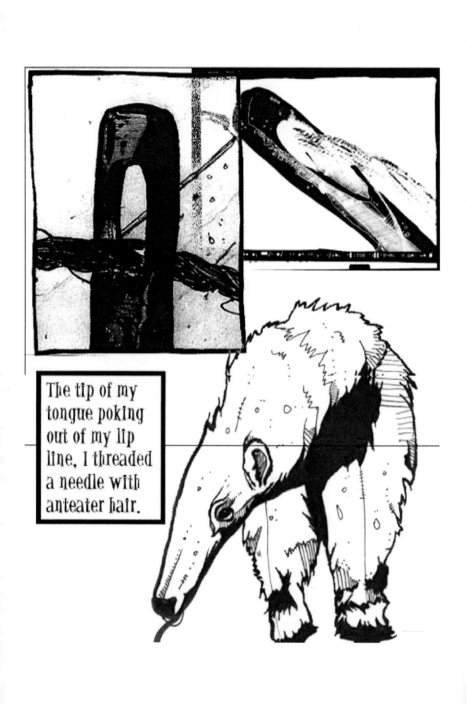

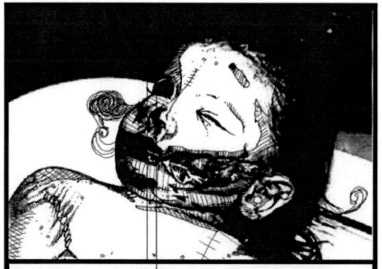

And the moment I finished sewing up my little sister, a stranger came along and kidnapped her.

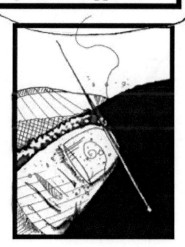

He painted her **FLORESCENT YELLOW** and stuffed her into a bird cage.

Overhead a giant buzzard's stomach grumbled like thunder

SOMEWHERE IN TIME

I climbed into a hole and dared somebody to follow me. Heated whispers. Then the crowd dispersed. I climbed out. Trees bent in the wind. Sand on my cheeks. A Xerox machine salesman ambled by carrying a Xerox machine on his back. I clotheslined him. I stole the machine and sold it to a golf club salesman for $65.99. We played nine holes. We made copies of our hands, exchanged the copies, and said goodbye. Hot today. 97 degrees and humid. Sweat soaked through my shirt. I took it off and hung it on a branch. I went to a shirt store. As I walked inside, a security guard tried to clothesline me. I ducked. "You need a shirt," he said. "But I haven't bought one yet," I replied. The security guard floundered. Three hours later I selected a shirt, purchased it, and clotheslined the cashier who sold it to me. I clotheslined the security guard for good measure. Outside a fire engine ran over two lovers on a Victorian tandem bicycle with one giant wheel in the front and one tiny wheel in the back. I picked up the bike and attempted to ride it, but the chain snapped, and the wheels deflated, and the handlebars fell off. I walked eight blocks. French subtitles formed beneath my feet whenever I spoke aloud. I asked a man if he would buy me a tin of sardines, for instance, and the subtitle said, "M'acheter veuillez une boîte de les sardines." He wouldn't do it. "Pourquoi," read my subtitle. The man shrugged and offered me one of his shoes. "Non. Merci. Je n'aime pas le goût des chaussures." It started to rain. I clotheslined a pedestrian and stole her umbrella. I ran to the nearest Bruce Lee amusement park. It stopped raining. Bruce Lees everywhere. Some of them mannequin robots. Some mere impersonators. Rollercoasters passed overhead emitting signature Bruce Lee squeaks, squawks, and hiyaaaahs. I bought a bag of potato chips and poured vinegar on them. I waited for the vinegar to sink in. I ate a chip. It tasted bad. I threw the chips away and went to see what was going on in the parking lot. Cement trucks everywhere. Drivers crouched behind steering wheels and ate lunch out of paper bags. One driver blew air into his paper bag and popped it. The other drivers weren't expecting the popping sound. Riot. Everybody emptied out of their cement trucks and attacked each other. A cadre of Bruce Lees exited the park and joined in. Spectacle of clotheslining. I escaped in a hot air balloon that delivered me to a cornfield. A farmer chased me with a scythe. I eluded him by nailing myself to a cross and posing as a scarecrow. Dusk. Dawn. I detached myself from the cross and went to a hospital to have my wounds treated. A nurse took off my shirt. I grabbed her wrist. "That shirt's brand new," I warned her. She shook off my grip and injected me with a sedative from a souped-up hypodermic needle. Sleep. Consciousness. Hunger. Anxiety. The cycle of life. I ran outside in a surgical gown. "They stole my shirt!" I went back to the shirt store, bought another shirt, clotheslined another cashier and the security guard. Outside the cashier's husband waited for me. He chased me for a half hour. We both got tired and went to a bar. I drank seven Pilsners. He drank three Rolling Rocks. I apologized for mistreating his wife, then destroyed a jukebox with a sledgehammer. I fled. I entered a building, climbed one story, and jumped out a window. I did it again. On both occasions I landed awkwardly but didn't break anything. Smell of cheap cigars. I looked over my shoulder. There was an ostrich. Smoke oozed from the thin nostrils in its bill. I sat on a bench and chewed off my fingernails. Tomorrow I was getting married. I called my fiancé and canceled the wedding. She told me we had gotten married last week. I told her I wanted a divorce. I recanted and told her I would be home late. Change jingled in my pockets as I jogged twenty miles to a cemetery. I walked around, looking for people whose names I didn't like the sound of, and clotheslined their gravestones. The cemetery ranger saw me and called the police. They came. They looked for me with metal flashlights. But I was long gone. I was halfway across Tennessee. A long state. A thin state. Like an arrowhead or a slice of mica. Everybody wore straw hats and drove Buicks. I only saw one red Mustang.

THE EGG RAID

A boy forgot how to fall asleep. "I can't do it anymore," he told his mother. She ordered him to go to bed or his father was going to hear about it. The boy said, "Oh yeah. I remember how to do it now."

He went to bed.

He stared at the ceiling and tried to remember how to fall asleep. Close your eyes—he knew that much. But then what?

In the hallway, somebody whispered in harsh tones.

The door creaked open and a butler appeared. He turned on the light. "I'm sleeping with your mother," he said. "We're running away together. She wanted me to say goodbye for her."

"Don't," said the boy.

Rearranging a bowtie, the butler nodded apologetically, turned off the light, and slipped out the door.

In the hallway, a curt shriek ... scuffling and grunting ... sucking noises ... The boy pulled the covers up to his nose.

The door opened and his father walked in. The boy

pretended to be asleep.

The father turned on the light and said, "I know you're pretending to be asleep. Your mother told me you couldn't remember how. By the way, your mother's gone. Everything's going to be all right, though. I ordered a blow-up mother to replace her. Well, that's it. Good luck with the whole sleep thing." He turned off the light and slammed the door behind him.

The boy flipped over and sobbed into his pillow.

In the hallway, a machine roared to life and labored in quick, methodic spurts . . .

The door opened and the father walked back in and turned on the light. He leaned a blow-up doll against the wall. The doll had a 1960s flip hairdo and wore a blue airline stewardess dress.

"Mom?" said the boy, springing to his knees.

The father arranged himself next to the doll. He removed a banjo from a long wicker case, got into position, and strummed a fast, friendly tune . . . Ten minutes later he abruptly smashed the banjo to pieces against the floor like an angry rockstar, then attacked the doll with a large kitchen knife, stabbing it over and over in the chest and screaming "Die! Die! Die!" until he had reduced the doll to a clump of mauled, ruined plastic.

"Excuse me, son," said the father, turning off the light. This time he shut the door carefully, quietly.

The boy lay flat and pulled the covers over his head. The extreme darkness beneath the covers scared him. He poked his head out into the open and peered at the ceiling.

In the hallway . . .

The door opened. Nobody came in. The door

The Egg Raid

closed.

The boy remembered something about sleeping. The next step. The step that came after closing your eyes ...

In the middle of the night, the boy awoke. Moonlight shone through a half open window. His father sat on the edge of the bed. "I can't keep doing this," he said softly. "Being your father, I mean. It's too hard. There's too much explaining to do." Groaning, he stood and walked into the boy's closet. "I'll be in here if you need me." He shut the closet door.

The boy closed his eyes to go back to sleep, but he had forgotten how to do it again. He got out of bed and went to the closet to ask his father for advice, but the closet door was locked. He went downstairs to the kitchen to get a snack, but the refrigerator was locked. He went back upstairs to lie in bed and think about things, but his bedroom door was locked.

He heard something inside ... the sound of a crow tearing flesh from roadkill ... The boy kneeled and peered through the keyhole.

There was a man dressed in his father's clothes. In place of his head was a giant white egg tilted to one side. "I am an egg man," he whirred. "I am an egg man and I commit egg raids." He sprinted toward one wall and crashed into it. He sprinted toward another wall and crashed into it. He sprinted toward the bedroom door and crashed into it. The boy leapt backwards on impact ... He got up. Tentatively he put his ear to the door and listened ... No movement, no sound. Nothing ...

Yolk leaked into the hallway ...

He opened the door and stepped into the bedroom. The door stayed open.

Turning on the light, he tiptoed across the bedroom, and shut the window. He tiptoed to the closet and looked inside. No sign of his father. He shut the closet door.

He tiptoed to his bed where the butler slept, soundly, using the mangled carcass of the blow-up doll for a sheet ...

STRONGMEN & MOTORCYCLES (& MONKEYS, TOO)

Well-mannered strongmen are hideous anomalies. Don't believe their polite handshakes, their nods of friendly affirmation . . .

I edit the sound of the daily news with a synthesizer and a pocketful of nitroglycerine. Nobody minds. The lights flicker. The night retreats into a bellhop's expectant gaze.

Dialup connection snapcracklepop.

The question is—why are muscles a prerequisite for strongmen? Strength is a relative term. Strength can indicate corporeal authority in equal measure with Einstein's motorcycle . . .

Vroom.

Screech.

Kachunk. Kachunk-kachunk.

To drape oneself across a motorcycle. To treat the machine like a chaise lounge, one leg dangling over a chrome handlebar as words ending in -*ly* pour out of my speechhole. A seagull shits on the muffler. I wipe it off with a shirtsleeve and tumble into the surf.

A strongman swims closer to shore and introduces himself. He tells me his name (Giovanni Belzoni). We make smalltalk. He comments on the saltiness of the ocean, the curls in his beard. He explains how much he misses the circus ...

Monkeys are perceptive. Monkeys are capable. Hence the expression: "Monkey see, monkey do." Nevertheless do not approach monkeys exhibiting solar coronas or inflated penumbra. The same goes for all simian organisms and some plant life ...

I have known strongmen who bludgeon idle circus-goers with rubber mallets. I have seen clouds evaporate into thin air.

I can tell you when the basement looks like the balcony—claustrophobic playgrounds of light beams and mothballs ...

P.O. BOX 455

As I searched my wallet, the postal clerk tore up the book of stamps. I asked to see the manager. The clerk removed another book of stamps from a drawer and tore it up. Before I could respond she destroyed a third book. Then she called over the manager and told him I was responsible.

The manager eyeballed me. "It's a federal offense to tear up stamps. That's like burning a flag. That's like burning your grandmother."

"I never set fire to anything that didn't deserve it," I admitted.

A trap door in the ceiling scraped open. We looked up at it. It scraped closed.

I blinked at the manager. "Shaving is a crucial part of robosapien culture. Where is the toilet please?"

"The toilet is government property," he said. "Are you a government employee?" The clerk swallowed a book of stamps. The manager looked askance at her, but he didn't say anything.

"Excuse me." I walked away.

The manager raised a finger. "Razors are not permitted in the post office! Come back her, sir! Security!"

A closet door rolled open. Inside an adolescent security guard in a tight-fitting uniform snored like a lawnmower. He snorted awake and lunged at me with a nightstick. I sidestepped him. The security guard fell onto his knees and the nightstick bounced off the floor and struck him on the chin. He cocked his head, unsure of what had happened, and slumped over unconscious.

In the restroom, a postman scrutinized a bald patch on his head. He quickly put on his hat when I entered, pretending to adjust it. I turned on the faucet of the sink next to him and lathered up my face.

"P.O. Box 455," whispered the postman. He didn't look at me. He continued to adjust and readjust his hat.

I ran a straight razor down my cheek and neck. "Pardon me?"

The postman's hands fell limply at his sides. "P.O. Box 455." His chin trembled.

"P.O. Box 455," I echoed. "What's in there?"

Now he looked at me. He covered his mouth, eyes round and gleaming, and shook his head.

I accidentally cut one of my sideburns too short and had to compensate on the opposite side.

On his way out of the restroom, the postman tripped over a garbage can. Stamped, unopened letters spilled onto the linoleum floor. The postman slipped on a letter and fell down. He slipped on another letter and fell down. This went on for two or three minutes. He reached for the doorknob each time before losing his feet beneath him. I observed him in the mirror. At last he was able to grip the doorknob and use it for leverage. Panting, he cracked open the door, glanced sternly at me over his shoulder, and slid out.

I splashed water on my face. I bent over and held my head under a hand dryer. It was a clean shave.

I stood, yawned.

There was a key on the lip of the sink. I picked it up and inspected it. The inscription on its bow read:

455

I ran a fingertip over the number. Dirt came off. Or oil. A black substance, in any case. I rinsed the key, blowdried it, polished it with a handkerchief, put it in my pocket, stared at myself in the mirror, blew my nose, and left the restroom.

Out in the hallway the entire postal staff awaited me in an orderly triangle, as if somebody had lined them up like bowling pins. The manager occupied pole position. He adjusted his belt several times and said, "Give us the key."

I looked behind me. I looked at the manager. "Is there a problem?"

The staff members shifted uncomfortably and traded annoyed whispers. The manager shushed them and readjusted his belt. "You know there's a problem," he said calmly. "The key. Now." He stuck out his hand.

"I don't have the key." I took the key out of my pocket and showed it to him. "I have this key. But this isn't the key you mean."

"That's the key," the manager said, pointing at it.

I returned the key to my pocket. "Anyhow, I'm on my way to the ... what is it called? The mailbox room? Is there another name for it?"

"We call it the key insertion room," said an anonymous member of the staff. The manager glared at her and reluctantly seconded the claim.

"Well. That's all, then." I walked forward. Carefully I weaved through the postal workers, trying not to touch them, pardoning myself if I did touch them. They regarded me with singular expressions of disapproval and enmity.

In the last line was the postman who had addressed me in the restroom. He hung his head and stared at the floor. I paused next to him. "What's in the box?" I asked.

His eyes pinched shut. He took a deep breath through his nostrils, tilting up his chin. His mouth twitched and compressed into funny shapes.

He fainted.

I went to the key insertion room.

An elderly security guard in a loose-fitting green uniform accosted me at the entrance. "You do it like this," he twanged, then stuck out his hand and made a turning motion. He demonstrated again. And again, and again. I thanked him and began to search for the right box. "Remember what I showed you!" he exclaimed from behind me, making another turning motion.

P.O. Box 411 ... 426, 427 ... 450, 451, 452 ... 455. I lifted the key and stuck it in the keyhole. I could feel the guard's breath on my neck.

"That's right," he said. "You're doing it. Good."

"Piss off, you old bastard."

The guard clutched his chest and staggered backwards. "That ain't nice! How'd you like it if I called you an old bastard?"

Apologizing, I turned the key and opened the box.

Inside was a figurine. Nothing else. I removed it. Examined it.

The figurine was about five inches high and made of hard plastic. It had limbs that swiveled at the armpits and groin, but not at the elbows and knees. No scratches, nicks or cracks. It looked normal enough.

I showed the figurine to the guard.

He gasped.

He pointed at the figurine. He pointed at me.

He clutched his chest again, staggered backwards again ... and collapsed like a stack of deadwood.

"Are you all right?" I nudged his chin with the toe of my shoe. He didn't move. I kicked him in the ribs. He didn't move.

I exited the key insertion room.

Postal workers either fainted or ran away when they saw me coming toward them holding the figurine in my hand like a PEZ dispenser. The younger security guard tried to punch me, but I dodged the blow, and he fell into an ungainly somersault and tumbled down the hall. The manager got in my way, too, although I clearly disillusioned him. "Are you going somewhere?" he asked. "You can't go anywhere. You've imploded. Every step you take is a step in the same direction." His Adam's apple quivered ... He dry heaved. He went cross-eyed ... He smacked his lips, motioning at the figurine. "You can only march in place now."

The trap door in the ceiling scraped open. We looked at it. It scraped closed.

I handed the manager the key to P.O. Box 455. The postal clerk tried to snatch it from him. He fended her off and gave me a free book of stamps. I thanked him.

As I left the post office, I entered the post office. There was a line. I took out my wallet and searched it. No money inside. No credit cards or I.D. Only a key. I removed it, inspected it.

At the front of the line, a gust of stampflakes shot into the air . . .

HOVERCRAFT

Dad stole a hovercraft and parked it outside the motel. Then he left us.

There was a note on the door when we got back from the supermarket. It read: "G'bye!"

Mom dropped the groceries in her arms and clapped her hands together. She dashed over to the hovercraft and hopped into the cockpit. The aft fans roared to life.

Tossing the motel key at me, mom pulled out of the parking lot and veered onto the highway.

I picked up the groceries and went inside.

The TV didn't work. I ate some cottage cheese with a plastic spork.

The next morning dad came back. "I was kidding!" he announced. He nodded at me and began to inspect the air conditioner.

I put on my clothes and went outside.

Another hovercraft was in the parking lot. I looked in the cockpit. Mom wasn't there.

The owner of the motel came out. A freckled, withered man wearing a sandpaper suit, he asked what was going on.

"Hovercraft," I said.

Suspicious, the owner approached the vehicle, leaned into its rubber underside, and began to scrape up and down. His pace quickened. Soon he had sanded a hole in the hovercraft. It deflated.

I started to cry.

"I know," said the owner. He squeezed my shoulder and went into our room. There was a gunshot.

Dad walked out. He told me he had changed his mind again. He frowned at the hovercraft, hotwired a station wagon, and drove away . . .

I went inside. The motel owner sat on the edge of the bed, clutching his stomach. Blood dribbled onto crinkled brown legs. He said he cut himself shaving. He stood. He fainted. He stood.

He staggered out of the room.

I crawled onto the bed and fell asleep. When I awoke the TV still didn't work. I followed the trail of blood outside.

The hovercraft was gone. In its place was an old Mazda RX-7. An anvil had fallen on its hood and smashed it into a calamitous U-shape.

The blood led across the parking lot to a cliff that fell into the sea. In the distance, a hovercraft jumped waves and did spinouts. The sun felt hot.

GIRAFFE

She had stuffed the shoulders of her periwinkle blouse with socks. She said she never wore socks anyway so what's the difference?

I found myself on the street, lying beneath a double-decker bus, staring at a rusty gasket set against an ominous canvas of fiberoptics. I blinked. I crawled out from underneath the bus, hailed a taxi, and told the driver to take me home.

"Where's home?" said the driver.

"Home. Home."

"Home," he reiterated.

At home, she tried to eat pasta without boiling it. She rested the long, hard strings of linguine onto a plate and stabbed them with a fork. "It's not working," she complained. "I can't pick it up." She stabbed the pasta with increasing angst until it had been broken into small enough pieces to nibble. "It doesn't taste the same," she noted.

I found myself on a rooftop looking across the landscape of the city. Spires, steeples, mirrored skyscrapers surrounded me in every direction. The sky was blue. On an adjacent rooftop, a giraffe stared at me. Its long, spotted neck buckled in the wind. But its gaze never wavered.

I jumped off the rooftop and pulled the string on my parachute just in time, although I skinned a knee, and I had to dive out of the way of oncoming traffic. On the sidewalk, I cut the parachute loose and bought a newspaper from a kiosk. I opened the newspaper to the business section. This picture was on the front page:

There was no title, no caption, no accompanying story. Beneath the picture rained the sharp columns of the stock market.

I walked home.

She had stripped the hides from all of the umbrellas and stitched together a vast cape. She demonstrated how the cape might also function as a flag, giv-

Giraffe

en a tall steel pole. Additionally, the cape could be used as a tent during jungle excursions. She set it up in the living room, using kitchen knives for tent clips, stabbing the fabric of the umbrellas into the carpet, urging me to pretend the walls were deep, dark foliage, a rain forest, full of monkeys and wild things and other preternatural beasts that had existed on earth for millions of years, that were prepared to eat trespassers even if their flesh disagreed with the most sensitive palate.

I found myself at the zoo. All of the zookeepers had been locked in the cages.

There were giraffes everywhere, immobile and quiet, loitering. I recognized the one from the rooftop. I tried to get its attention, waving my arms. But it didn't see me. Or ignored me.

I stroked the giraffe's leg. It made a chirping noise.

The zookeepers pleaded with me to set them free. I said I would have to think about it and went to use the toilet.

When I came out, she was waiting for me.

She had climbed atop my giraffe and was trying to ride it. "Giddyap!" she shouted, thumping platform heels against its belly. The zookeepers cheered her on.

The giraffe swatted her with its tail. She flipped backwards over a fence. A loud crash preceded a tsunami of curses. She climbed over the fence, caught her dress on a picket, and somersaulted onto the asphalt with a great tearing of fabric. She stood, dazed. She realized she was naked from the waist down and tried to cover herself. She yelled at me, insisted it was my fault. Everybody watched her quietly—giraffes, zookeepers, me.

I told her it wasn't what I had imagined. She asked what I meant by that. I said she knew what I meant and we should leave it at that.

She accused me of breaking her heart. I apologized.

I said goodbye.

I climbed onto the giraffe and whispered into its ear. It loped out of the zoo.

The other giraffes followed us. We made our way through the city in a long, proud parade. People gathered on the sidewalks. Soon it was a full-fledged extravaganza, comparable to New Year's Day. As the applause and cries of joy grew louder, I leaned my cheek against the soft neck of the giraffe, closed my eyes, and conjured images of home.

HOUSEGUEST

I was tossing a boy in the air when the houseguest broke in. The boy fell through my arms and landed on his head. He stopped giggling. He turned pale and went limp.

Somebody down the hallway screamed like a plane crash.

I ran upstairs and armed myself with two survival knives I kept in a shoebox beneath my bed for these occasions, then went back downstairs, tentative, vigilant ... I spotted the houseguest. Tall and lean, he stood in the foyer and held a survival knife in each hand. He wore a weathered veteran's jacket and had slicked-back gray hair.

I threw a knife. It sailed end over end and struck the houseguest in the neck. His head snapped back and froze for a moment. He dropped his knives. He waved his arms as if trying to maintain balance on a tightrope.

Slowly he turned and paced out the front door.

The boy crawled into the foyer and told me he was going to turn me in to the police for child abuse.

I said, "You have that right. Good boy."

I left.

The houseguest moved down the sidewalk. Occasionally he tripped over his feet and fell into a parked car, then pushed himself up and slogged on. The knife remained in his neck, plugging a terminal jugular.

I said, "Stop."

He stopped.

Without turning, he raised a trembling hand and made his fingers into a hang-loose sign.

All of the neighbors were cutting their yards. They turned off their lawnmowers and stared at us as if we were a car crash happening in slow motion.

I threw the other survival knife at the houseguest. This time I missed.

The lawnmowers growled back to life.

The houseguest removed the knife. Blood fell from the wound like streamers of unraveling crepe paper. He held the knife in his hand for a moment, caressing the worn leather handle with a thumb. Then it slipped out and clanked against the cement.

I went back inside.

The boy was gone. He left a note on the floor. "Dear Parent. I'm running away. I took some soup and crackers from the pantry. I will send you a check for these items when I get a job and make enough money. *Auf Wiedersehen*," said the note.

Upstairs somebody turned on the shower and flushed the toilet at the same time. The lights flickered. The house hiccupped, shook.

I opened the guestbook and ran a finger down the guest list. There was only one name.

The name had been crossed out.

The doorbell rang. I opened it.

Houseguest

It was the houseguest. He looked different. His hair had come undone, and there was something about his face. He stood there, pale and limp, clutching his neck. I invited him in. I ushered him into the kitchen. He collapsed onto the dinette table and his hand fell from his neck, exposing a gash that whistled like a deflating tire.

Snapping on a pair of dishwashing gloves, I carefully dressed the wound.

THE TRAUMATIC EVENT
OR
THE WALRI HOLOCAUST
OR
THE HAIRY DEED
OR
THE MAN WHO DISAPPEARED

The Latin term for walrus is *Odobenus rosmarus*. Translation: "Tooth-walking sea horse." I read this in an encyclopedia. It was a traumatic event.

I captured a walrus and put it in my freezer. It froze.

I shot a walrus and put it in my basement. It bled out.

I put a sleeper hold on a walrus, skinned it, and put on the skin.

Another walrus tried to seduce me. I took off the

skin and beat it to death with a crowbar.

Another walrus figured out what was going on and tried to run away. I pursued it in a Volkswagen Rabbit and ran it over.

I took a sip of bottled water.

Ten thousand walri drowned and melted in a deluge of boiling oil. I stood at the top of a cliff, hands dirty, manga eyes flickering . . .

A friend suggested I buy a pet walrus. I kept it for a week. I fed it. I groomed its hide and mustache. I took it for walks. I polished its tusks. I bragged about it to the neighbors, read it bedtime stories . . . The walrus barked and spanked its fins at the conclusion of my puppet show. I removed the puppets from my hands, bowed, cocked my head, frowned, frowned . . . and cut the walrus in half with a two-handed executioner's sword. I dumped the halves in my friend's driveway with a note taped over the walrus's face. It read: "Friendship is an excuse for hairy deeds."

In the aftermath of traumatic events, victims often demonstrate "extreme" behavior. The events revise selfhood, desire, personality . . .

. . . walri stampeding through the jungle. I launched missiles at them from a military helicopter ripping across an orange sky . . .

"Tell me about that dream," said my therapist.

I nodded. "Which dream was that again?"

"You know. The one about the walrus."

"Oh. Of course. It's better if I show you, though." I stood and opened the closet. A walrus shuffled into the office. Rolls of fat formed on its neck as it angled up its head and looked back and forth at the doctor and I.

"Apropos," I said, raising a finger . . .

Things got out of hand and I accidentally slaughtered the doctor, too.

They arrested me.

I refused to post bail—perfect waste of a trust fund—and spent three weeks in prison eating ginger nuts and lifting weights and making friends. I wore a suit to my trial and hired Sam Waterson as my lawyer. He wore jeans and a tattered Harley Davidson T-shirt, but he made a convincing argument on my behalf. The jury acquitted me with unanimous applause and delirious grins.

I hugged Mr. Waterson.

On the bleached white steps of the courthouse, I noticed a herd of walri chasing a double-decker bus down the street. I tailed the herd for six blocks until the bus tipped over and the walri invaded it. I killed them before they could do anything to the passengers, then saved the passengers, escorting them from the wreckage one by one. Moments later the mayor handed me the keys to the city. Flashbulbs popped. "Thank you, Mr. Soandso," intoned the mayor. "Thank you for that hairy deed. You are truly a good-intentioned and thoughtful soandso. I hereby . . . "

I hugged the mayor.

I indulged a delusion of grandeur.

I used a key to open a manhole and disappeared forever.

GUNPLAY

I heard gunplay.

I opened the door of my room and looked down the hallway.

There was a man with a hole in his chest. The hole was on fire.

I closed the door. I opened it and looked out again.

There was a man in a ski mask cradling an elephant gun. He stroked the muzzle like a woman's thigh. He removed his mask and stared at me. His jaw had been torn off. I saw the distended epiglottis in his neck cavity dangling beneath a row of horse teeth.

I closed the door and turned on the TV.

There was only one channel. In the featured sitcom, a man with a white beard purchased a red balloon from a balloon vendor. The helium leaked out immediately. Laff track. He explained what happened to the vendor. The vendor encouraged him to buy another balloon. He did, a blue one. It deflated like a Whoopee cushion. Laff track. The vendor said, "Sometimes it takes three times to get something right." The man bought another balloon. Green. The vendor popped it with a syringe. Laff track . . .

D. HARLAN WILSON

I turned off the TV. Two men in gray leisure suits had entered the room. They stood in the corner and observed me for a long time. Slowly they turned and observed each other ... One man began to stab the other man in the chest with a butcher's knife. The victim didn't scream or cry or struggle. He let his attacker kill him, politely, admitting only twice how much it hurt.

A woman with long blond hair in a skintight dinner dress and shoulder-length gloves rushed into the room and admonished the killer for not paying enough attention to her at the party. The killer ignored her, stabbing his victim with methodical precision until he slid to the floor, emitted a meek croak, and died ... The killer grabbed the woman by the elbows. He shook her, screamed at her. He threw her onto the bed, tore off his clothes, yanked up her dress, and made love to her. I pretended not to see them. Occasionally I glanced in their direction.

Somebody knocked at the door. I opened it.

"Room service," said a man holding a semi-automatic pistol. He wasn't wearing a mask. His jaw was intact.

He stormed inside and shot holes in the ceiling until the killer and his mistress snatched up their clothes, opened the window, and threw themselves into the sky.

I closed the window and drew the shades.

Satisfied, the man pointed the pistol at me and fired. It was empty. He continued to pull the trigger. He put the barrel of the pistol to his temple and did likewise.

It fired. A tentacle of gore reached out of his skull

Gunplay

and sloshed against the wall. Bewildered, he stood there dumbly ... and collapsed. He fell to his knees, his head bounced from shoulder to shoulder, and he slumped onto the corpse of the killer's victim.

I covered them with the bed sheet.

Somebody had turned the TV up too high next door. I pounded on the wall and urged them to turn it down.

I heard gunplay. I couldn't tell if it happened on the TV.

There was a knock at the door. I opened it.

A diminutive bellhop asked if I wanted my bags taken downstairs. I said I wasn't leaving. He asked for a tip. I gave him five dollars. He told me a long joke and clarified the moral: "In life, we must make fun of death *ad infinitum*. Because death will always have the last laugh." He smiled and asked for another tip. I said I didn't have any more money. He scowled.

There was a knock at the window.

"Excuse me." I shut the door. I went to the window and opened the shades. It was the killer. I opened the window.

"Is he gone?" the killer panted, studying the room.

"Who?" I replied.

"The man in the hallway."

I went to the door, opened it, and looked down the hallway.

There was a balloon vendor. The colorful bouquet of balloons floating above his shoulder appeared to be attacking him, diving down from the ceiling and thumping him on the head. A few balloons popped and dirtied his face with powder. He swatted them away like flies. Then he unfolded a pocket knife and—

I shut the door and told the killer that I didn't see anyone. He climbed back into the room, complaining about relationships. "Never fall in love," he intoned. I said I would make coffee. But I only had decaf.

There were dead ladybugs in the coffee bag.

"I don't drink coffee anyway," said the killer. He took a long shower. I waited for him to finish, inspecting my face in the mirror for imperfections.

He got out, toweled dry, and asked if I had deodorant. I retrieved a stick of Old Spice from my toilet kit.

"I prefer spray cans. I don't want to roll this substance across my dark places." He gave it back to me. He put on my suit.

I heard gunplay.

The killer made a gun with his finger and thumb and blustered into the hallway. "Lock the door!" he exclaimed, and shut the door.

I opened the door.

There was a police officer in an English Bobby hat. He had also made a gun with his finger and thumb. He and the killer pointed their fingers and fired silent blanks at one another, pausing to cock and recock the hammer of their thumbs.

Their fingers unexpectedly went off at the same time. Their heads exploded into hydras of sparkling brains.

I shut the door. There was a woman on the bed. Brunette. She had taken off her clothes and spread her legs. "Let's pretend we love each other," she said.

"But I do love you," I said.

"But let's just pretend," she reiterated.

"I know how to do that."

"You are capable. You are free."

"I am what I want to be."

"Nobody knows what they want to be. Ergo—" She removed a sawed-off shotgun from underneath a pillow and aimed it at the TV.

I paused ... "There is ointment in the bathroom." I couldn't think of anything else to say.

She opened her legs wider.

I went into the bathroom. As I searched for the ointment, I disavowed the corpses that somebody had crammed into the shower stall, and I evicted the sound of gunplay from my ears ...

HOG RIPPING

"I can rip just about anything in half." I started with a sheet of vellum followed by a slice of cheese. Neither feat garnered much acclaim, so I moved on to a quarter, a picnic basket, and finally a hardcover edition of *War and Peace.*

Spectators observed me with bovine expectancy . . .

"What about this here hog?"

The farmer pushed his way to the front of the crowd. He removed a choke chain from the hog's neck and kicked it in the shin. He kicked it again. The hog crept forward, glancing nervously over its shoulders. Occasionally it emitted a subdued oink.

I knelt and clicked my tongue. The hog came closer. I reached out my hand. It sniffed and licked my fingers.

I stood and circled the hog, gauging its distribution of poundage. Most of the weight appeared to be in its haunches, although its oversized head gave me second thoughts, and its potbelly commanded my attention, too. I looked into the hog's eyes. It oinked at me assertively.

Hog Ripping

I lifted the hog over my head and ripped it in half. Offal exploded across the sky like the pulp of screaming watermelons ...

"My hog!" shouted the farmer, falling on the carcass. He struggled like a child to cram the swine's entrails back into its severed halves. "I loved this damned hog! It was a prize hog! God help me!"

The crowd became unruly, but their tempers weren't beyond repair. Things didn't really start to get out of hand until a slot technician dared me to rip his vending machine in half ...

ELBOWS & VESTIBULES

How he denied the existence of elbows. How he engaged the machinery of tall vestibules.

A bridge made of Cornish hens.

Stitched together at the legs and wings, the hens had been neglected and gruesomely overcooked. And yet they each exhibited textbook quotas of rosemary. Still, as I began to cross them, their collective skin flaked, splintered, cracked ... Chunks of fowl plummeted to the river of conveyor belts below.

I took myself by the elbows and ushered myself to the wayside.

THE BURN

It burned ...

The curtain hummed into the ceiling and exposed a grocery cart. Theatergoers stiffened in their chairs.

The grocery cart inched forward. It squeaked across the stage, spitting suitcases, toilet kits and garment bags out of its chainmail belly. Bellhops rained from the roof beams. They nailed the stage and clambered after the treasure ...

A theatergoer's walkie-talkie came to life. He put it to his ear and listened to a voice.

"It burns," the voice whispered ...

The grocery cart squeaked to the edge of the stage and toppled into the orchestra pit. Tubas and maestros sprung into the air as if off of trampolines.

Theatergoers slapped index fingers against palms for thirty minutes ... Fatigued, they climbed into Mini Coopers, sped up the aisles and out into the city. An usher sealed the theater doors behind them with a blowtorch.

The bellhops dropped the baggage they had collected and screamed for the audience to come back and tip them. Their throats shredded into long ribbons of spaghetti, and the curtain fell onto the stage with a wet thud.

The usher lit a cigarette. He took a puff, exhaled, and slowly twisted the ember of the cigarette into his palm.

It burned . . .

TO BED, TO BED—GOODNIGHT

I marched into the kitchen and dropped my suitcase onto the floor. It exploded. Dirty socks and frayed underwear sprung onto the appliances.

"I'm home," I announced.

"Where have you been?" asked my mother, blowing steam from a cup of chamomile tea.

"Everywhere. I am a world traveler. I have seen everything and met everybody. A snake tried to bite me once. A cobra. I outran it. Now I'm back."

"Where are you going?" asked my father, blowing steam from a cup of lentil soup.

"To bed, to bed—goodnight."

"Goodnight," said my parents as steam swallowed their heads and melted the cone of their throats ...

Kyoto circa 1888

D. Harlan Wilson is an award-winning novelist, short story writer, literary critic and English prof. Visit him online at:

www.dharlanwilson.com
dharlanwilson.blogspot.com

Lightning Source UK Ltd.
Milton Keynes UK
UKOW051151100112
185091UK00001B/69/P